There's a pastiche of moments in a Metro Goldwyn Mayer production where all the flowers in an endless field suddenly surge into technicolor and begin singing; a chapter by a Dutch psychologist in which the commonplace nature of miracles is given its due; Metcalf's evocations of abandoned battery emplacements off the coast of Marin; flights of music by Sondheim and Satie; seemingly throwaway scenes in a novel by Hammett where a city's dizzying infrastructure opens via a hole in the pavement; Einstein's meeting with Satan under a streetlight in Cambridge as told by Buzzati; any number of Serling sequences that have stayed with you for years after having laid their deep strain of groundwork for morality. Similarly you will identify so completely and on such a personal level with Allen Frost that you may resent any characterization of the work as a fiction as it walks you through, sentence after glorious unexplained sentence, often to places that are left hanging in air, implying their trust in you to complete them.

Frost is indeed traveling here in the company of kings you may or may not recognize in the interactive sessions of a logic that derives as sweetly from a concept of unified physics as it does from the image of a woman ultimately liberated by snails she endeavors to teach.

—Tom Kryss, author of *The Search for the Reason Why: New and Selected Poems*

Other Books by the Author

Ohio Trio: Fictions (Bottom Dog Press 2001)

Bowl of Water (Bottom Dog Press 2003)

Another Life (Bird Dog Publishing 2007)

Home Recordings (Bird Dog Publishing 2009)

The Mermaid Translation (Bird Dog Publishing 2010)

The Selected Correspondence of Kenneth Patchen, edited by Allen Frost (Bottom Dog Press 2012)

BIRD DOG

PUBLISHING

THE WONDERFUL STUPID MAN

FICTION

ALLEN FROST

Bird Dog Publishing
Bellingham, Washington

Bird Dog Publishing/ Bottom Dog Press
PO Box 425, Huron, Ohio 44839
Lsmithdog@aol.com
http://smithdocs.net

Credits:
General Editor: Larry Smith
Cover Design & Back Cover Photo: michael paulus
Additional: Farrin N. Abbot, shutterstock/grafvision
Line Art: Allen Frost
Layout and Design: Larry Smith
Font Style: Sylfaen

Two of these stories first appeared in
Little Engines #4.
"Aristotle's First Car" has been nominated
for a Pushcart Prize.

THE WONDERFUL STUPID MAN

For 3 Rays:

Ray Bradbury
Raymond Carver
Raymond Chandler

Aristotle's First Car

When the old man in a gray toga appeared before my desk, clutching the prop-like new edition of *Poetics*, of course I half-thought it was a gag. "Whah?" I managed to gasp at the apparition as I stood up.

I couldn't understand his words torrenting out at me, but his gesturing all the while between himself and the book made his meaning clear.

Now in my line of work, publishing, entertainment is really what it's all about. And good entertainment equals money to be made. That's the business. I won't say I've read Aristotle before, maybe once in school, I don't remember, but he continues to sell after all these centuries. People continue to buy him. So a light went on as I watched his act. He was good. What the heck? I decided the return of Aristotle wouldn't hurt.

"Alright, alright," I drew my hands flat through the air. "Let me think..." This fantastic thing presenting itself to me, I just needed to figure out what to do with it. With him, I mean. There were things I had to know since communication with words was so hard. I leaned into the intercom button and asked the secretary to have my car ready for me out front. "I'm taking my lunch," I added.

Aristotle—yes, I had already begun to think of him as genuine—nodded and followed me out onto the office floor. The clerks and busy bodies watched us cross their midst and order an elevator. Nobody spoke a word though, and we were soon on our way down.

Aristotle seemed no more alarmed by the elegant contraption we were in than a seeing-eye dog. When the door slid open to a new scene, he took in stride that he had just traveled between worlds.

We passed through the lobby crowd and I led him out the revolving door to where my car was parked at the curbside.

A brand new Chrysler Cordoba, gleaming long and wide and white awaited. I opened the door for him, motioned with my hand for him to sit inside, then when he was comfortable, I shut the door and went around the front grill to my side.

Aristotle was quite taken with the car, the tinted sunroof, blue interiors, including the fine Corinthian leather upholstery.

He gasped at the golden key that started the engine. I turned the wheel and we were off. The 8-Track music came at us from all around. Aristotle watched me drive so intently, as if it were the most incredible thing he'd ever seen. I laughed a couple times at our absurdity.

When I stopped next to a curb a few songs away, I explained how he could open the car door. He nodded and brushed his toga legs outside.

After I put some quarters in the meter, I led him along the pavement beside the shiny storefronts. He was still babbling, and of course I couldn't understand him, but all that was going to change very soon, I hoped.

Nicholas was open for lunch. A woman carrying a plastic bag opened the door and passed us. She gave us a look that Aristotle didn't catch—he was staring in wonder at the café window.

He shouted something, delighted by the poster of the Acropolis, the lettering on the glass, the smell of lamb, the growing olive branches, the whole miraculous familiar vision.

I laughed at his response. I opened the bell sounding door for him.

I didn't see Nick, but his wife and her sister were watching us. They were never friendly to me, not like Nick. They wore black and made sandwiches and strong coffee behind the counter. They spoke Greek.

The sight of me with Aristotle sparked their interest though. Brushing their hands off on their aprons, they both washed up to the counter edge to observe.

Aristotle approached them sincerely, talking happily and gesturing all about in the air.

The two women began a slow conversation in their Greek with him. It went back and forth. They warmed.

I took a seat at a little table where I could watch them. He showed them his book, and I smiled at their reaction. This was perfect, I was already scribbling down ideas on a napkin. I had big plans for him.

After a while I stopped writing and I got up to see how they had progressed.

Aristotle was popping olives in his mouth and had just accepted a plate of delicate pastry. "Uhh...Aristotle?" I had to interrupt them. "We have to go." I tapped my watch.

The women actually beamed at me. I never saw that before, not even Nick's good humored show ever caused them to step out of their cold.

Nick's wife spoke to me for the first time ever, "You bring your friend back soon, okay?" The sister passed Aristotle a plastic bag filled with Greek treats. Maybe he would share, I'd not gotten around to eating.

"Did you like Aristotle?" I dared to ask her.

They nodded, very pleased, but they were finished talking to me. They gushed out some goodbyes to Aristotle who waxed eloquent.

I had to pull the guy by his toga to get him off stage, out the door.

He was laughing to himself, in such good spirits, swinging his plastic bag of take-out.

We got settled back in the car and I fit the gold key he liked so much into the ignition. Big plans...

"Oh!" I didn't have my notebook. I pantomimed for Aristotle to stay put, I would be right back.

He was busy gnawing and feasting, blissful.

I hurried onto the sidewalk back to Nicholas. A giant in a cloak held the door open for me.

My notebook and pen were waiting for me where I left them. The two women were busy with a man in black, but I waved to them as if we were old friends, and so I got what I forgot and left again.

Tucking the shape into my suit pocket, I slowed down and stopped beside a parking meter. Stepping out into the middle of the street I looked up and down both ways, but what was the point of searching? The car and Aristotle were long gone.

A FACE IN THE INDUSTRY

Pal Tack turned off the television after his name went by in the credits for the third time. Yes he was famous, yes he had been doing his program for over forty years, but it was time to relax now. He was back in the tall hotel tower, he could return to normal, nothing needed to happen when he was off the air.

Reaching upwards, he touched his chin and pushed his head to the left. It turned smoothly all around in a full circle. Around again, this time Pal caught his ears and unscrewed his head off the rest of the way. Uncorked from the rest of him, his eyes targeted his face towards the fish tank set on the table seated next to his bed. His body bent him towards it like a swayed oak tree, and then he dropped the head in. It made a small splash.

Pal's features were suspended in the blue thick liquid. Some bubbles were stuck around him. After his hands tossed a black curtain over the tank, his body could lay flat across the bed.

The room in his suite became very quiet, the only sound the ticking alarm clock. It would wake a long time from now, at six in the dawn.

The window looked out from the 48th floor. The city below was hidden by a layer of fog. It scratched up against the glass but didn't make a noise.

The clock worked its way through another hour before something finally happened.

There was a loud knock on the door, two raps, enough to snap the eyes open in the lead colored embalming fluid.

Alerted, Pal's body lurched to a sitting position, his arms flailing in the direction of the bedside table as the door jerked open.

"I've been thinking about what you told me..." said the big silhouette of the station president looming in the doorway. He took a step into the dark room. He was trying to adjust his eyes to Pal's commotion on top of the bed.

Pal snapped a newspaper open in front of him like a big gray moth unfolding wings.

"Now, don't say anything yet, Pal." LBJ let himself in and closed the door. He paced into the deep carpeting. "I want you to know how I feel, I want you to understand my point of view, why it took me some time to come to this conclusion." He made a noise like a whale breaking from deep salt water. "Who would have known it would come to this. I mean, we've been watching you for half a century. Almost..." He paused. "I know you say you could go on for another fifty years, and don't get me wrong, you've done us all a favor, you've kept our ratings going and you've made a face in the industry..."

Each time he looked at Pal, he only saw the newspaper, with the legs stretching out from underneath the wide paper. Pal's hands gripped each side tightly, all his ring fingers holding a kind of sail on top of the bed.

"I just wish..." LBJ continued, "I just wish you could see it our way. Here's your chance, you have an anniversary show tomorrow night. You have a big media push, millions of eyes watching, so why not step out gracefully and say goodbye?"

A rattle waved across the newsprint.

"What?" LBJ leaned over the bed. "Wait!—!" The moonlight showed all the words upended. "You got that thing upside down, you read it that way?" He chuckled explosively and had to wait to talk again. "That's funny! I gotta tell the board about that. You've got style, Pal. You're one of a kind!"

He slapped a hand around Pal's thin trouser cuff. "You think about what I said." He turned around and padded across the carpet to the door. He looked back over his shoulder before he left and laughed. "Reading the newspaper upside down! What a character!" he howled, then he left the room.

Pal's chest rose and fell. As his arms dropped to his sides, the newspaper sighed down and made a shroud across his lank form. His head wouldn't let him rest though. It called urgently to be let out of the tank.

The bed creaked and newspaper crackled as he reached and took the curtain off the fish tank. He dipped one hand in to fish himself out.

The room door burst open, LBJ yelled his way into the dark suite with the film crew. "Just kidding, Pal Tack!" as cameras and lights flooded on. "We—"

It was a dreamy freeze of time. They were all caught in a web for a moment: the two men with the camera and lights, LBJ, the crazy statue of Pal Tack holding his head. Then when they snapped back, they came back hard.

The camera and lights fell with a crash and pitch black as the crew fainted to the floor. LBJ managed some sort of croaking chop of a loud word, and Pal Tack urgently reassembled in the dark.

LBJ slapped his hand along the wall looking for the light switch, cursing, finding it, bringing sight back to the room.

Pal blinked at him out of unison.

"What in...?" LBJ stared at him. He kept a hand on the wallpaper by the switch, as if to steady himself. "Was that—" he stammered, "some kind of trick? You—" he forced a laugh. "You can do magic? I mean..." He noticed the two crumpled men on the floor. "I mean you don't have a head! Your head was gone! What's going on, Pal?!"

Pal was silent. In a sort of ecstasy, his head had soaked up a good third of the fluid. He could feel it pouring down back into the many channels of his body.

LBJ leaned over and grabbed the film camera off the floor. "It's all here. We saw it happen." He let out a laugh again as he stared at the camera. "We were making a little jokey film for the big show tomorrow. I would say, 'Pal you're not hip anymore, you're going to have to bow out of the business,' then surprise! 'We were just kidding!'" He glared at Pal, "But your face isn't even attached to you! What *are* you?!"

Pal was sitting on the edge of the bed. He was still filling with the youthful flow. Until he was restored he didn't feel like talking or moving.

"That's great...I'll just have to figure this out. We can't have a star whose head comes off," LBJ stalked over to the telephone. "I have to make some calls, I need help on this." He picked up the receiver, dialed and looked at Pal while he waited. "How long has it been this way? You're not even real."

While LBJ turned away to talk and write on a notepad, Pal stirred. He rubbed his hands over his smooth face. After a stretch, he got to his feet.

LBJ was oblivious, his voice went on like a metal fan in the corner. With that noise in his ears, Pal walked over to the door, stepped over the unconscious couple, grabbed his coat off a hook and quietly left the room.

It was late. The door shut behind him, and his leather shoes crushed the carpet across to the elevator. The brass doors opened and he was in.

As he rode down, he smiled at the syrupy muzak. He remembered introducing that tune to television thirty years ago, when it was a song for teenagers. Now it was a thousand violins gliding him on wings to the lobby.

The drop left him rubbery and when he left the elevator at the ride's end he loped out like an astronaut, until he found his gravity again, halfway to the hotel entry.

There was a vacuum running behind the counter. Pal tightened his coat about himself. Nobody saw him leave.

He took a deep breath of the eucalyptus blue night. The gardens in front of the hotel flowered in the bright lights. It was sun all the time for them.

Though he had nowhere particular to go, Pal felt an urgency to get there...at least out of the glow of the big streets. He guessed his secret was out. Even though the evening was heavy with perfume, warm and languid to move in, he had to be on guard from now on. Who knew what LBJ was planning now that he was in control?

Into the parched space between streetlamps, Pal cut across the road to the other side where a stand of palms was growing.

It was amazing. It was like he was being watched over by angels, the way he made it so easily into the blackout under the tall trees and leaves.

He laughed out loud. The first sound he made after the treatment always sounded so loud and weird. He coughed and caught his breath.

"You got away, pal."

Pal jumped.

In this place barely out of the long shadow of the hotel, there was a camp set up—a tent and the embers of a small fire.

"Nobody'll find you here, pal. This is the invisible world."

But Pal didn't feel invisible when even this forgotten man knew who he was. "I have to go," Pal told him quickly.

"Alright friend, good luck," the man called after him as Pal mashed through the fern cover and flower stalks.

Breaking through the last of the park, he saw the dark backs of old buildings with an abandoned lot stretched in between him and them. Pal found a rent in the chain link fence and crossed an open sea of cracked concrete and garbage.

He liked the looks of the brick shape in front of him. Sleepy and left untouched for ages. There was even a fire escape clinging to its wall, woven and tangled as rugged ivy.

He pictured himself up there away from the world where he could catch his breath and think of a survival plan.

In no time he was climbing the alley shadows up the metal ladder. The thing rattled with his steps, its rusted voice warning him higher into the air.

Pal and the stairs stopped on a landing next to a locked door. With his ear to the cold, he gave a listen to the murmur inside. He smiled. Anyone born in his age would know what lay behind. Going in there, you could get lost for hours.

He sat resting his back against the movie theater bricks. "How am I going to get out of this?" he sighed. Music patched with sound effects lapped on the other side of him. People were watching people in a fantasy. It was comforting. That was his life—or what used to be. Now that he was cut off, it would be harder than ever to return.

As he stretched his legs across the grillwork, he yawned, crossing his arms on his chest, feeling sleep riding near. Reviving so suddenly without a full treatment and then all the excitement and running had made him very tired. His heavy eyelids dropped, opened and dropped again for the rest of the night.

"He can't just disappear!" LBJ bellowed into the telephone. Pal's hotel room was a riot of clues spread out for officers, detectives, and worried dark suits from the television station. Chaos. "We all know his face and if he takes it off to hide it we'll just look for a guy walking around without a head on!"

LBJ's voice railed on in the sky while 48 floors sharply down and drawn away in the wind of rushing carriages and morning crowds, the trail of Pal Tack ran...through leaves, dew, over concrete, onto a wall, pulleyed to a high spot on creaking iron.

A noise like mechanical birds stirred the famous man.

He was woken by the tinkers in the alley below. He turned onto his side to watch down the grill. Going through the new trash before the garbage trucks arrived, the tinkers had found treasure and filled their wooden wagons.

Pal coughed. He took out his little cellular phone and dialed the number of his hotel room.

"What now?" he heard LBJ's hoarse voice.

Pal smiled, there was all sorts of noise in the background.

"What? Who is this? Pal?! Is that you? You crazy headless nut, get back here! I'm not—"

Pal cut the connection with his thumb, then laughed and coughed and dropped the phone.

The coppery thing spun away like a fishing hook. He could only watch helplessly until it hit and broke on the alley stones. This was the first time he had woken with his head on in years. And there was no tank full of fluid to rush into him. He felt feeble and sore from a bed of rivets and beams.

With great care, he found each step and let himself down the long way to the ground.

The effort actually drained him. He wanted to be gone, unseen by the time the garbage trucks arrived but he was moving so stiffly that it was all he could do to get out of the alley, around the corner before them. Dream slowness dragged on him.

When he made it to the faded sight of a wooden telephone booth, he slid in like a ghost and closed the folding door while he sat.

Slumped in there with collar turned up, he regarded his reflection glassed between the paint peeling trim.

He was aging. There were cracked lines in the skin on his face. He stared at the seams cut into him. This was someone he never had to think about...At least not since his operation some twenty years past. The synthetic amniotic fluid had kept him preserved. At home among all that youth on TV, he felt like he could fly with them forever. With each new song craze on the charts they danced—they kept coming to him and flowing around him. Weren't they a river that never ended and couldn't he stand in them forever? But what a different picture looked back at him from this glass frame. At last, in the space of a day, he was old.

Pal found a credit card in his pocket and hoped it would still work in the telephone. He prayed he hadn't become a non-entity so soon. He fed it into the phone. It had no effect on the dial tone.

So that's the way it is.

He needed to use quarters. He was lucky that he had a dollar's worth in his pocket.

There was no point in another crank-call to LBJ. No doubt Pal Tack would become the man who disappeared overnight.

Pal dialed a number he knew from his generous charity contributions. Maybe Pal had always felt some deep sort of empathy for them. They couldn't help growing old. Even when he was different from them, he cared. They would help him.

After a few rings a voice stepped in, "Gray Panthers, Los Angeles Chapter. This is Betty, may I help you?"

"Betty," Pal croaked. "It's Pal Tack. I'd like to talk to Herb if I can."

"Of course Mr. Tack—You…Are you alright?"

He couldn't really say anything. How much did they know? He hadn't seen any news.

"I'll get Herb," she hurried.

Pal had been on good terms with Herb for years. For a while they used to golf together every weekend.

"Pal? Herb here. Do you need help?"

"I do. I need a favor."

"Of course."

"You need to get me out of here, Herb."

"Yes, of course. Where are you? Wait, let me find a pencil—Betty, where's the paper?"

Pal Tack remained in the phone booth. He had found a good place to wait. Around him was the decay and fade of a neighborhood that had turned to a ghost. It was funny that he would end up here and funnier that he would feel at home.

By the time a pale yellow Cadillac parked next to the phone booth and three elderly men and women got out, Pal was creaking. He waved a sorry windmill paddle.

Herb clasped Pal's arm. "Pal, what's happened to you?"

"I'm in a little jam."

"We've heard. The film on TV—"

"It's not real," Pal cut him off.

"Well, of course!" Herb agreed, acting surprised. Then he pointed, "Come on, get in the car, we'll take you to the landing."

Pal didn't feel like talking during the ride. He kept his eyes shut. Picture the Fountain of Youth, see it in your mind's eye, he pressured himself, and hurry. The car was air-conditioned. He sat in the back seat and listened to the Perry Como tape while Herb drove.

When they got to the parking lot of a five story cannery building, Herb announced, "There it is."

Up on top of the flat roof poised a silver autogyro.

They all got out of the car and Herb signaled the air machine to warm up. A roar of exhaust flapped the rotors into revolving.

"You sure that thing will get me to Mexico?" Pal asked.

"Don't you worry about it, Pal." Herb shepherded them closer to the rattle. They felt some of the warm breeze.

Pal could still keep up with the Gray Panthers, stiff as his knees were, following Herb and his companions to the padlocked entrance, but he knew he was living on borrowed time.

Herb keyed it open. "This building is sort of our secret hideout."

"Last month we had a square dance here," Betty chirped.

"Yeah, well we use it for other things too," Herb made clear. The room they were in was still strung with rainbow banners from that dance, dipping in the heavy amber crawl of dust from the ceiling fixtures. Floors above them, the autogyro rang like a tin locomotive. "Come on," Herb urged. "Up these stairs..."

Herb opened a metal door and they saw the stairway when the lights went on.

"Oh boy," Pal let out.

Betty laughed and patted him. She showed him her purse, "Look, I brought some disguises. But you don't even need them. You look just like us, dear."

"We're glad to have you too, Pal," Herb smiled. "We're strong, we have the advantage of numbers."

"And we vote," she added.

"Well, if you can get me to safety, I'll never forget you," Pal promised.

They each took a hold of the handrail to help them climb. They were merry until the third or fourth set of stairs when they all started to tire. Herb stopped at the next landing so they could catch their breath. "We're nearly there," he puffed. "What's in Mexico anyway, Pal?"

Pal shook his head, "Let's keep going. That thing up there is making an awful racket. Probably half the city hears it." This is my third body, he told himself—surely I have more strength than four Gray Panthers! I have to hurry before I'm gone...

Pal moved past Herb and finished the last set of stairs to the door. Watching them labor towards him, he scolded himself, *I'm not like them, I can still be young forever, I just need to get to Mexico.* He put a trembling hand on the exit door handle and pushed.

When Pal opened the door, the hot oily prop wash forced in. It was so loud and forceful that Pal felt one of his teeth drop out. Frail in the doorway, he would have fallen if the others hadn't grouped around him and guided him into the sunlight.

A door on the autogyro popped open and they aimed Pal for it. The tar on the old roof peeled away from the gust in stripes.

Herb yelled something in Pal's ear as they tucked him into the machine. Pal heard the word "Mexico," but he couldn't unscramble the rest. He waved limply and shut the door. He felt like a lost soul.

It was about half as quiet inside. There wasn't much room. Pal was seatbelted next to the pilot, all the flying controls cramped against his knees and a foot away the glass curved over him.

Suddenly the pilot lifted them straight up into the haze and Pal had to close his eyes or blackout. The sight of the roads and block after block of city tangled and sparkled below, he couldn't watch. He tried to picture something in his mind, but nothing would form. If only he could convince himself, I'm in the dark, on the stage...The lights have dimmed for a brief commercial break...and when I open my eyes there will be plenty more music and fun. Soon, everyone will see me again...

A SPELL OF BAD THINGS

Before the 4 o'clock news interrupted the music, she turned the radio off. She didn't miss hearing about the war, she would rather listen to the steady buzz of electricity strung around the place. Karen Bindle had another hour to go in The Music Store before she could turn off the lights overhead and those bulbs in the window display would go dark. It was Thursday evening after rain, and cars were slipping past her door on their way home.

Even though earlier she had sold piano lessons to a mother's daughter, that fact hardly made it worth her while to be here all day. Still, after all the day's time, there was only 53 minutes to go.

What could she do but run her life through and through while she leaned on the counter and watched the cars glide in the glass. It felt like a spell of bad things swept her along. Sometimes, it seemed all too often, her worst thoughts would come true, as if she wanted them so.

She managed 4:30 by straightening all the lesson books in the rack: saxophone, clarinet, trumpet, violin and the lone book on tuba on the end that nobody ever looked at.

When she supposed it was safe to tune in the radio again, she was right. Some jazz played "It Never Entered My Mind." If anyone asked, she could show them the sheet music for this song. Over there, under the green window sill.

The door barked open and she looked up to see what looked like a magic act winding in, a sort of mechanical toy in the form of more than twenty students and their gray-haired teacher who was trying to keep them together.

Karen shot a glance at the clock to notice it was ten minutes before five. She watched the teacher approach her.

The teacher kept swatting at the students and in a way, with all that flapping motion, she sort of flew to the counter and landed elbows onto it heavily.

Karen was a little afraid of the woman's black rimmed eyes and heavy posture, almost a hunchback. She's just tired, Karen tried to be kind, minding all those children.

"Can we rent instruments here?" She hurried her words, "Do you have enough for a whole marching band?"

Karen said, "Sure." She laughed. The Music Store had won the lottery. Who counts every tragedy until the last moment when it's going to be the end, then turns it all around? In a kind of dream, with movements that seemed photographed, Karen pulled open the drawer and took out the ledger.

"You wouldn't believe what a day we've had," the teacher told her. "It's hard to do a show with no music." She was filling out a checkbook.

It felt like a hurricane pulling down everything from the shelves, making piles in front of the counter, inventory that kept disappearing. By the time Karen had cleaned the place out and added matching sheet music for four different songs and returned to the counter to tell the teacher the amount, she was exhausted. Karen felt bad in the pit of her stomach that this woman would have to pay such a fortune, but apparently the teacher didn't mind at all.

Karen took the check from her hand and stared at all the numbers for a long time before she caught herself and trapped the payment in her pocket.

It was 5:07 when the marching band left, leaving the store emptied of stock.

In the stun of all the buzzing lights and emptiness, she reached for the phone. She wished there was someone she could call to tell. Well anyway, she smiled, I have myself to know and congratulate the miraculous event.

And I'm not coming to work tomorrow, she cheered herself. She got a paper from the waste basket and wrote 'Closed Friday' on it in crooked block letters. They didn't look so cheery so she drew a smiley happy face. It looked like a pumpkin a week after Halloween, but she carried the page to the front door glass and taped it on so the message faced the street. She turned the display lights off and hit the main switch too. The store shut like a clam, dark except for the pearly glow of the lamp back on her desk.

She let herself out the door into the evening, locking the keyhole behind her, even though there was nothing in there to blow wind into.

On the other side of the street, she couldn't avoid the warm gold colors of the Mexican restaurant on the corner. Sometimes she went there after a bad day. This time was different. She looked both ways and waited for a chance to run across. The smallest people were driving the biggest machines she'd ever seen. When there was a break, she held her arms out like a dervish as she ran across the tar. The road was still a little slick from the day of rain. It reflected the yellow lights she ran towards.

Bursting in the door beside a painted Mary statue, she waited awkwardly next to a cactus. There was a No Water sign on the cactus. She thought about that.

It was busy. Two waiters passed her carrying plates to crowded tables. She picked at her fingernails while she waited for them to come to get her.

"Buenos noches, senora!" His grin genuinely surprised her. "Smoking or non?"

"Oh," she said. "No, I don't smoke. I never have in my entire life."

"This way please."

She followed him to the corner, the back wall, a table beneath a white round clock and the fierce looking scene of some bandits in an old photograph. She sat, then accepted the menu with a clucking thanks.

Across the dining room out the big window rippled the mirage-like blur of her darkened music store.

She started to tell the waiter her lucky story when he reappeared with salsa and chips, "I have an amazing story," but when she looked into his eyes, she worried about where her words were going. She had this trouble sometimes with men. Nervously, she covered up her start, "Oh, it's not over yet though," not too sure how to go on. When she quickly put a tortilla chip in her mouth, he went away.

"What am I worried about?" She mumbled to herself, "I'm a new person, everything is different than it was." She dug into the maroon colored pocket of her coat to take out the check. It was real wasn't it? Of course.

I could cash this and go to Mexico tomorrow if I wanted to. I could take that waiter with me, she smiled at her thought. *Well, I could!*

"Are you ready to order?" he had reappeared.

"Oh!" Her shadow bumped across the banditos on the wall. She clawed up the menu, "I'll have what I always have. The #5. With chicken."

"Very good."

He took her menu away.

She uncrumpled the check and reminded herself. *I could go far away*, she thought. *I could go somewhere sunny. There's nothing stopping me but me.*

While she ate chips, then her meal, in the brassy sound of her thoughts, the rain began falling again on the street. Everything out there slipped, and tipped reflections whirled off traffic and bright lights.

She took out her checkbook to pay the bill. Before she filled in the date, she looked up at the clock as if it told all time.

The second hand was moving backwards, then it stammered and began to move clockwise as if it had been caught doing something wrong.

She hurried the rest of her check, signed it and squeezed out of the booth.

The rain and wind slurred up against the glass door. She pushed her way into the night, into sight of a police car parked against the curb directly across the street. Her breath caught in her. She listened to the restaurant door bang closed behind her.

Two officers were shining flashlights into the windows of The Music Store.

With all the hurried terror of a blowing paper bag, she gusted over the road. "What's wrong?!" she gasped when she got close enough. She couldn't see what they were looking for. "I'm the owner, is there something wrong?"

"Are you Karen Bindle?"

"Yes, what's wrong?"

They edged towards her. "This store of yours is suspected in participating in a large transaction of musical paraphernalia." There was a cop on either side of her.

"I don't understand. What's wrong?"

"You better come with us, Ms. Bindle. In the cruiser..."

They locked her in the back, she watched them through a steel mesh while they drove, slashing in the rain. "Can't you tell me what's wrong?"

The radio crackled with codes and backwards sounding speech. "We'll *show* you what's wrong, ma'am," the driver told her. His eyes in the glance of the mirror riveted on her. Then his partner muttered something into the radio.

Karen worried and held the tough hide of the seat as the cruiser skidded a corner. When she saw television shows like this, she would quickly change channels—she had no interest in being here.

They traveled on a road that clung to the winding bends of the Skagit river, the wide black scree of water that rushed from winter mountain peaks. Wherever they were taking her was some distance from the comfort of the city. She worried herself into a picture of her walking in the moss and heavy drip of the forest cedars where no doubt some terrible sight was awaiting. She looked down at her thin canvas shoes, hugged her arms tightly and worried more about what her bad thoughts knew.

True enough, the farmhouses and valley land turned into a tall wall of trees, and soon they were driving in a plunge of darkness. The river was always out there, every once in a while she caught a glimpse of its extra black wake covered in white chops of rapids scratched by moonlight. She grew scared.

The cruiser pulled off the road onto a smaller one-lane road. The tires chewed into gravel and bumps and holes, then slowed.

She held her hands, she felt dropped into Sleepy Hollow.

At last the headlights shined out over the banks of the river and the car stopped at the bouldered edge.

The police let her out. The air was so much colder than in town and each little breath she took hurt her like a drink of glacier water. The deep feeling of these trees...unlike the parked boulevard trees they were shaggy with cat-tail moss and lichen, and they rocked and watched her, alive as bears.

"Follow us. This way..."

Their flashlights took her towards the roar, cutting along the forest floor.

She saw where they were leading her—it was masked with flares and police shining battery lights. In an eddy where the river dug and shallowed a pool against the crumbling roadside, a school bus lay smashed and nearly submerged by the icy water.

The policeman made sure she didn't fall as they slid down the rocks and silt to the stone bed.

She could see the fiery glint of brass instruments laid upon the corrugated shore with the bodies of children run out of air.

"Ms. Bindle?" One of the cops tugged at her sleeve to start her walking again.

"No," she said.

The other policeman moved on over the slippery stones, leaving them behind.

"I can't."

"Listen Ms. Bindle, do you remember anything about who was with the children? There's no sign of the driver or the teacher or whoever was leading them. Would you be able to—"

"No."

The river was so loud her ears drowned in it and it filled her head with rushing. She couldn't speak anymore. A spotlight fished across the rapids. Across from her in the current was a French horn with a little hand holding on.

The Puzzlebird

Drew Pederson pointed his scarred finger at it and warned me, "That's the Puzzlebird. Don't go near it."

I wanted to. I wanted to go right up to the cage and look at it, but this was my first night at the station, I was learning the ropes. Still, before Drew took me out of the oak paneled room, I had to ask, "What's it do?"

"They use it for predictions and surveys. I don't know, elections and stuff."

"Don't they use computers for that?" I asked.

"Just don't mess with it. Come on."

I followed Drew but it was hard not to think of the Puzzlebird. I would have to come back later to check it out. At the end of my shift when Drew was gone I'd be getting my relief to go home.

He opened a gray door into the hallway, and we went into a dimly lit room barely bigger than a closet. There was a stool surrounded by three walls of buttons and dials and only the door behind us where we came in.

"Here's your clipboard," Drew said, taking it off the hook and passing it to me. I got a good look at his finger again. A white scar circled round its width.

"All you gotta do is monitor the equipment. See? Check the levels and write them down twice an hour. Like this one here…It's #5. Take the reading and you write it on the clipboard under #5 at—" he glanced at his watch, "10 PM. Cake? Right?"

"Sure," I nodded.

"Alright. You get two ten minute breaks at 12:15 AM and 4:15 AM. You take lunch after your 2 AM reading. But don't forget the 2:30 reading. They already told you how important this job is when you were hired. Any troubles, you pick up that phone. Any questions?"

I didn't have any questions. It was like any other job. Better than most I've had. The whole thing was my responsibility. That means something after so many years of having a boss watching over my shoulder.

"Alright, see you."

He was gone. It was just me. I sat down on the stool. I felt like someone flying in the middle of downtown skyscrapers at night, all the little yellow windows blinking on and off in a hum of electricity. The clipboard had a pen attached. I wrote my name, Roberto Santos, at the top where the blank was.

Who reads this anyway? I wondered. Unless something goes really wrong, it all just piles up day after day.

I took the first reading of my shift. I wrote down all that matters. Then I had a half hour to sit and do nothing. In this cramped place. Tomorrow I'll have to bring a book.

I started to think. First I thought about my girl. She's sleeping now. Last job I had it was the same deal. Nightshift. I used to go home in the dawn and pluck garden flowers for her while I walked back to her apartment. I'd have a wet handful of dew and petals and leaves, sneak up the stairs, open the door to her, go across the quiet wooden floors to her doorway. She sleeps in purple. Oh, how I would take off my clothes and surprise her with me and my barrio flowers.

Then I looked at the clock. I had to. Only five minutes have gone by remembering her.

Here I am. A new job. I hope it will work. Who knows? I think about my lucky start with a word from someone who knew someone who got me in here. Eighteen minutes until the next count.

The Puzzlebird returned to me. What was that thing? It didn't even look real. I'm sure it was a fake bird. And the way Drew Pederson got all strange. Give me a break, I've grown down the alleys, I've learned what to believe and what is shadows. I don't have to be afraid; I know what to leave alone.

I waited until 11 PM. I watched the lights click across the walls. For ten minutes I fell into a trance watching them. The monitor board was connected to something alive like those machines in hospitals wired into patients. Televisions all over the city and for miles into the distance were bringing those signals into late night rooms, soaking people with the glow and stories of shows. I couldn't even tell what the station was programming. The message was coded by hypnotizing little lights.

At 11 I stood up with the clipboard and started recording in a clockwise direction. By the time I got it all written down, another thought had crept back into me. It wouldn't wait. I had to take a look at the Puzzlebird before the next reading was due. I left the clipboard on the stool.

When I edged into the hallway, I made sure there was nobody around, then I went quickly across to the other door.

Opening the door slowly so I could take a look in— Empty—I went inside.

The Puzzlebird was in the cage. The cage sat on top of a metal cabinet against the wall. It looked like a toy from here and getting closer didn't make it look any more real. I whistled at it to make it move or something, then I tapped the iron cage with my finger.

The Puzzlebird flashed off its little swing and chopped its beak down on my finger tip. I shrieked, a white rip of lightning pain shot through me. I tried to fling the thing off but my finger was caught between the two bars. It wasn't real, the Puzzlebird was some kind of cruel trap.

I couldn't free myself and I was bleeding into the cage. I had to call out, "Drew! Hey! Anybody?!"

That's when I saw there was a latch turning on the side of the cabinet. It spun halfway and like clockwork some maniac sprang out, screaming and laughing or crying all at once.

He leaped around me, ran over and kicked the wall, then came back to me and laughed right into my face.

"You saved me!" he yelled and laughed again. "What day is it? I'm alive again!" he slapped me on the back and I howled.

I looked at my finger. The Puzzlebird had dragged my hand across the cage some ways.

"What's it doing? What's going to happen?" I asked.

"You're going to be the new Puzzlebird." Then he got sad for me for a second, "Don't worry though. They'll tell you what to do. And then some day someone will replace you. You'll be free like me!" He got glorious again and ran around the room.

"Can't you help me?!"

The Puzzlebird was out of the cage, holding onto the cage with magnetic grip and pulling me towards the open door of the cabinet. That's where I would really be working.

Gathering Snails

She showed up at the same course early every morning, when there was still fog coming in from the sea, to clean the greens before the golfers arrived. The wide clouds blew off the ocean, climbed over the mountains and fell as rain on the fields, the nuclear power plant, and the growing town. The flashing headlights of the waking cars moved on the road she had taken there. Japanese lanterns with blinking light bulbs, swinging orange and pink and blue overhead, were the only light as she worked. She wore a sweater for this cold.

Sometimes newspapers flew in during the night, or school kids would sneak in to drink beer, leaving behind cans, batted by the windmill at the fourth hole, or half sinking in the stream.

Always there were snails on the course, somewhere. Water fed all the plants and the snails crawled in the green before the dew evaporated. Carefully, she would pick them up by their shells and drop them in the grass field on the other side of the fence. Beyond the metal fence were woods and farms and then on to the ocean, with so many waves in between, on the way to land again. Just like the tide, it would take the snails all day to travel back through the chain link, so she could find them all over again. Something in them endured. Silently, they would always come back to her.

Not long ago, all this land had been fields and trees, but in 1973 a farmer outside of town had a midnight vision of a Disneyland for golfers. There were sculptors flown in who turned cement, chicken wire and neon paint into his dream. Huge reptiles, a grandfather clock monster, a walk-through Mount Rushmore, an orange Buddha, and a fishing Humpty Dumpty formed the skyline. She had passed by them all her life. For her they were as natural there as the mountains further off in the distance. But she never expected she'd have to work there.

To pass the time in her glass booth, changing money into tickets and passing out putters, at first she used to watch everything so very carefully, impersonating a detective with her brown eyes. "You can always tell a lot about the people who come here," she would talk to her reflection in the glass. Just beyond was a dipping violet dinosaur. She tried to make her voice sound like television, pointing, "I can always pick out the first timers. It's the look in their eyes, their excitement, they could have been struck by lightning. So dazed by their surroundings and whether it's real or not…The complete opposite of the veterans." Working there watching from dawn to dusk, her mind stuck with thoughts, minimum wage hours passed slowly.

One morning, out of boredom with her job and her life sitting there, she started to paint letters on the snails she retrieved. Carrying a paint can and a small brush, she drew mornings and spent the rest of the day in her booth, wondering what would be on the lawn tomorrow.

Nothing about the golfers interested her anymore. Calmly, she offended people she had seen many times before by showing them how to hold the putter correctly. She looked the other way while someone tried to set The White House on fire. Truthfully, everything about this job spelled nowhere and she knew it and she steamed to herself, "I'm caught, surrounded by stupid people doing stupid things."

While the rest of the day disappeared, she would try to find meaning in the random arrangement of the snails. She kept a notebook, trying to break their code. Weeks of learning to use the alphabet, keeping careful observations of it all in her blue notebook, and it seemed that the snails could only sometimes line themselves up correctly in attempts to become a word for her. Teach them, she decided, instead of giving up. She learned patience with them, bringing their antenna shy faces up to her lips, enunciating to them softly and plainly, "A...B...C...D..." before setting them free. Twice, she caught herself humming alphabet songs from PBS as she walked between them, becoming their mother.

Snails were all she took seriously. All that brought her to work was the thought of them and at night she prayed for them. While she tried to sleep, restless, tossing, she looked through her window. The sky, the stars and constellations, sometimes the passing red lights of airplanes, it could all be read too, if only she knew how.

After a long night of raining, the clouds were leaving east when she arrived for work. She was tired from watching out the window all night. She opened the padlock on the booth door latch and stepped inside to punch the time-clock. Then she got the pail to clean the littered golf course. A paper streamer wrapped against the bridge and she walked in that direction, keeping an eye on the snails each time she stepped.

Her feet went over their mixed up language, plucking their curved yellow shells out of the lawn. It could have been any other day, but this was the day they talked to her. She found the word, QUIT wriggled next to her foot. With dew on the shells, the advice crawled purposefully for her to see.

She took the message to heart and got back in her rusted car. She slowly pulled out of the lot. There were places she had always wanted to go. She had just been waiting for the right time.

You're Always Right

Crumdecker never rode an elevator. He walked briskly, guiding his wife towards the door, telling her rapidly, "Always take the stairs."

"For God's sake, Randall, I'm not climbing to the 10th floor!" She stopped and ground the heel of her shoe in front of the door.

"Just come on," he hissed as he opened the door.

"No! Forget it! I'll meet you up there, I'm taking the elevator." She spun away from him.

"What are you doing?"

"What does it look like I'm doing?"

"You're not taking that elevator."

She pressed the button again. She ignored him.

"You can't do that, Gretel. I've told you a hundred times what—" he stopped as the elevator doors opened. "You're not getting on that elevator!"

She waved at him and got on the elevator. The door closed as she pushed the 10th floor button. This was the first time in years that she had been on an elevator. She forgot about how it felt when you shot into the air; she had to laugh and grab at the handrail.

Crumdecker stood there for a minute more, he just couldn't believe what had happened. Mumbling, he opened the door and went into the stairwell where his chiding words echoed around like a wind tunnel.

The doors of the elevator opened for the 10th floor. She was laughing. She stepped out onto the thick carpeting like someone recovering from a pie in the face. "Ra— Randall!!" she called. Then she remembered, it would take him a while to climb all the way to the door beside the elevator.

She could just picture Randall, walking all that way cursing her stupidity and growling every sensible thing he would have to say to her when he got to her. Then she had a terrible thought. "Of course," she smiled, still imagining him, "You're always right..."

"98%..." Crumdecker scowled. He was having to pull himself, using the handrail like a lifeline tied to the slant of a mountain. "It's a well known fact. Haven't I told you a million times, Gretel? What don't you understand?" He went up and up. The door with a 9 painted on it went by. The 10th door floated like a dirigible before him.

His breath came heavily. He put an arm against the wall. "You're lucky," he told an imagined Gretel, then he took the door handle and opened it.

Gretel fell in at him like a dying swan, holding her hands tightly on her throat, panting, "The elevator got me!"

And Crumdecker was so shocked he stumbled backwards, missing a step, turning upside down and caterwauling, waterfalling to the 6th floor.

He needed to be stretchered out to an ambulance. He needed a week of black sleep in a hospital, bandaged from head to toe like a mummy. By the time he could open his eyes and speak, a month had passed. His wife sat by the bed and worried over his life and death for hours and hours.

His voice rattled at her. She stopped staring at cut flowers. She got close and listened to him.

"I told you not to take the elevator."

She waited for him to say something else.

Do Orgami

The stack of origami books on his kitchen table shook from the rumble of the subway. Its yellow windows flashed past like cards being shuffled. He kept his eyes closed while it went by, then when the last car was gone, he opened his eyes. The room had returned to candlelight.

He was holding a folded piece of paper. Before the train appeared, he had been in the middle of Step #3 on page 49. The crumple dropped out of his hand. It lay on the table like a wrecked creature on Dr. Moreau's island.

It was impossible to learn origami with a subway tearing by the window every five minutes.

He was glad when the phone started ringing. "Hello?" he answered with weariness.

"What's the matter?"

He recognized the grainy voice and told her, "This apartment is too much. Is it time for the meeting yet?"

"Sure. I'll be there in ten minutes."

"The sooner the better. Oh—Barbara?"

"Yes?"

"Is it blue night or green?"

"It's red!"

"Oh yeah."

"I can't believe you, Fes!"

"I know, I know, it's a miracle I can think at all in this place. This is a million times worse than living by the highway."

"You'll get used to it. Look where I live."

"Yeah," he laughed.

"Thanks, Fes."

"Oh, sorry."

"I'll see you in ten minutes, okay?"

"Sure."

"Red," she said and hung up.

Fes left the kitchen into a little room next to the icebox. He could have stepped into the icebox, there was that little space. There were clotheslines strung, hung with seven different rainbow suits. He picked out the red one, slung it onto the hammock behind him.

"Hey!" screamed a shrill voice from the rocking chair.

"We have to get ready."

"Get this cheap suit offa me!"

"Okay Milo." Fes picked up the bright coat and revealed the ventriloquist doll on the hammock.

"What? Is it red night again already?"

"Yeah, I guess so." Fes slipped into the suit. Then he turned around and got the smaller red suit off the hanger. "Put this on. I need some coffee..." He tossed it next to Milo who cursed and swung and raged like an angry parrot.

In a few steps Fes was back in the kitchen and looking through the cupboard. He took out the coffee and spooned some of the black crystals into his opened hand. It had been a week or two since he had water. Coffee was rough this way, the stuff tasted awful dry.

He stood by the window and looked into the inky void between subway trains. Nothing to see, he could have been marooned in a cave on Pluto.

"You done, Milo?" he called.

The shrill doll replied, "Of course not! I need some help here!"

"Okay."

As he returned to the doorway he heard the doorbell. It had a flat sounding bell attached to it. "Oh," he said and reached to open it.

Barbara stood there holding her doll, Dottie. Her doll's eyes stared at him then looked up at Barbara, "He remembered," Dottie said.

"Where's Milo? I'm double-parked." Barbara was in a mood.

"Don't let them in here!" Milo shrieked. "Beat it, Dottie!"

"Hah!" Barbara's doll squawked.

"Would you hurry up!" Barbara said. "We'll be up on the street in the car."

"Okay, okay." Fes waved them off and went to get Milo.

Milo had the little suit coat stuck over his head, sleeves and pants tangled like telephone cords. He looked like a cardinal netted by the hammock.

Fes dressed him, scooped him up roughly under his arm and on the way through the kitchen he blew out the candle. The low rumble of the next subway came at the window like a moon on skates, emerging from an eclipse.

The auditorium echoed heavily with their clatter. A red tide of men, women and their fidgeting, shoving dummies filled all the chairs.

Barbara had been telling Fes about her new electric horse, going on and on about it, but he wasn't really listening, he was watching the remaining drops of rain roll off of Milo. Then she and everyone else quieted down when the lights dimmed.

The curtains parted and four elderly men made their way to the table at the center of the stage. Their feeble dolls held canes as well. The eight of them sat down and blinked at the crowd.

A man cleared his throat and spoke into the microphone, "We have a lot of things to get to tonight."

"Here we go," Milo groaned.

Fes put his hand over the dummy's clacking jaw.

The old man continued to read his speech.

"Aah!" Fes shouted as wooden teeth bit into his hand.

"I can't take it, I tell you!" Milo screamed.

Fes wrestled him. Barbara and Dottie and the others sitting around him were stirred and uttering.

"Everything's okay," Fes promised. "I'll be right back," he touched Barbara's knee as he arose and left her side.

Milo was shouting out any words he could get through their struggling up the aisle, out into the lobby.

Fes shook Milo, "Are you nuts!"

"What?! What now?"

"What are you doing? All we have to do is sit through it quietly. Just an hour and then we're free."

"I can't handle that garbage, that's all! It's a waste of my time!" Milo snarled.

"Okay, Milo, I didn't want to do this but you leave me no choice." Fes dug in his pocket and took out a roll of tape.

"Whaa?"

Fes wrapped it over Milo's mouth, around the wooden head a couple of times. Milo's top hot fell off and Fes leaned over to put it back on, then they returned to the auditorium's doorway. "Sorry, Milo," he whispered as he pushed the curtain to let them in again.

He had to stand there in the aisle, darkness blinking at the spotlit stage, blindly trying to find where they had been sitting with Barbara and Dottie.

The microphone voice of the old man reached him, "Maybe our late visitor can get the evening started. I'm sure you have something to entertain us with. Come down here to the stage, introduce yourself to us all."

"Ohhhh…" Fes groaned. The chuckling of his dummy buzzed behind the tape like a wax harmonica. Fes squeezed Milo very tightly with his arm.

As they walked leadenly down the aisle, a hand stretched out to him and Barbara waved a piece of paper for him to take. "Do origami," she whispered.

REAL YELLOW

When the moon came out of its bowl of white clouds, shining bright through the window of the tenement, Bertram Fenn woke up with a start.

"I've got it!" he said out loud.

Beside him, his wife groaned, curving back to sleep.

For days he had been trying to figure something out. Trust the night, the mystery of dreams to find his answer; he wanted to tell his wife but she was already asleep. He wasn't even tired now and he had to tell someone.

He slipped out of the thin summertime layer of blankets and searched the gloom for his clothes.

"I figured it out," he mumbled while he dressed. "Hah!" he beamed, pushing arms into sleeves, stepping his legs in next.

Bertram stood there in the pale blue of the room wearing his gorilla suit. It was his second skin. He wore it every evening on the stage. Putting it on now, he didn't even think twice—it was that natural to him. So he went padding out into the dim hall, down the stairway, outside.

He did laugh when he realized, looking out at the cobblestones, the gas-lit lamps, through the round holes cut in his mask. Still, at this hour who would see him? He wasn't going far, only crossing the street to his partner's apartment.

He loped over to the tall limestone building opposite, but his gloved hand couldn't open the door. Of course, he realized, it's locked for the night. Undeterred, Bertram slouched to the alley and the fire escape leading up.

Laundry, blank sheets and all sorts of ghostly clothes hung pinned from the ropes webbed between two walls overhead. Stars were everywhere. He had to stand there for a minute to watch. A pleasing breeze blew down his angry cut snarl. He saw the flash of a shooting star hitting the atmosphere and skidding out into sparks.

Then he started to climb, first the step ladder, then the metal steps. His heavy leaded feet took him echoing and shaking to the slant next to his partner's window. By accident, he knocked a potted plant off the sill as he reached a hairy arm inside.

"What?!" a silhouette shot up in bed.

The shadow of a gorilla spread across the moon colored wall.

"For God's sake, Bertram," his partner croaked. "What are you doing? Climbing around the city at night—it's three o'clock!"

"I know, I know, listen. I made an amazing discovery." The gorilla sat on the edge of the bed. "It's about Houdini."

His partner moaned, "That fraud..." and glared at the ape.

"I've been watching him close for a week and I finally figured it out."

"Figured what out? There's nothing to—"

"I know how he's getting out of that safe they lock him in."

"Oh Bertram, anybody knows—"

"No, this took me all week to discover his secret. Allow me to illuminate." With his giant hand, he pointed towards the ceiling. "I thought it had something to do with all the padlocks they put on the door, but that isn't it. It's so much simpler. The safe has a sliding panel! He just gets out like that!" Bertram clapped those hair-covered hands in triumph.

His partner shook his head, "Wrong!" Then he lay down again. "Now get out of here. Go back home and go to sleep."

"I know how his act works! It's not real magic."

"He's a fake, Bertram." His partner pulled his pillow over his face and that was it, he had disappeared.

Bertram couldn't stand the silence of the room anymore. An apish long sigh and he was clambering out the window again and the slow descent down the fire escape to the bricks, upset with himself for having come all this way before dawn.

Bertram fumed, "Maybe Houdini is an act, a hoax, a show, but who am I to say in the middle of dreamtime?" It was something everyone wanted to believe. They wanted it real even if there was no such thing. Letting out a yell made him feel better. What did it matter? Sure, he became the animal he played, howling again as he held to the bars and swung among the sails of laundry and outer-space.

This Home of the Count

The cape poured off his shoulders, over his pear shape as he clopped down the hall. His eyes were downcast to watch the floor, the way to the door he shared with the janitor. There was still another name written on below that, the name he always looked at proudly while he took out his keys: Count Misfit.

This home of the Count would be no more. It was a late-night loss. Instead of the shadowy drums of mystery islands, castles and candles and outer space creatures, the station only wanted to play commercials for shady enterprises. After midnight, they didn't want dreams, they wanted money.

The door opened to a cluttered space, like lifting the hood of some car abandoned on the side of the road. Broom-sticks crossing mops with mud colored tops, yellow buckets on burnt squeaky rollers, squat bottles of bleach and pink chemicals.

He shrugged and took off his cape. He hung it forever on the gold hook on the back of the door. It swung folds, then settled its shadow flat on the wood. No, he quickly decided, he had to take it with him, so he lifted it off and stuffed it under his shirt to bring home. It belonged to him.

The little mirror duct taped to the wall showed him the Count's face. Pulling his bat eyebrows off, he spoke, "Goodnight my friends, I can't see you anymore." Even though he was disappearing into the seams of night, he hoped that his image would become a haunting television ghost hovering in the dark spaces between channels.

Taking the rest of that face off, rubbing his skin until his character was gone, Earl Ray emerged and reached next to the sink for a paper towel.

The water running from the faucet made a silver sound. While it splashed, he dried off. The cuffs of his shirt were wet. He smiled at the fan letters pinned and taped on the wall. There were some loyal people out there in the watching world. He freed them and lined the pocket of his coat with them.

While the janitor was still upstairs getting coffee, slow to start his shift, Earl thought to leave him a last favor. There were a couple plastic gourds of cleaners on a high shelf. He emptied some of each into the yellow bucket with steadied hand. He tied a hose into the sink faucet and turned the water over hot.

Bubbles and steam gushed the bucket full until he turned the faucet off. He propped a mop into the white foam, then pushed the mop handle like an Italian gondolier, making passage into the still hall. The jerk over the jam slopped a wave onto the linoleum.

He stopped it and rested the handle at a crooked angle to the wall, under the KGUS framed fame awards. There was no picture of Count Misfit next to the beaming weatherman or fearless anchors.

Earl ducked under the drawn curtain and pushed the exit door open. A wave of night washed him as he stepped into the dark lot. The door clicked behind him and he blinked to work his eyes.

The best thing about the war was the blackouts. With the bright lights outlining the city blinded for the first time in so many years, all the stars could be seen. They shined above carefully, as if at any moment they might have to disappear.

He tried not to think of anything as he left the station. He listened to his shoes scuff the cracked concrete. The sidewalk along the way was aglow with the bright fullish moon in the branches. A fresh breeze touched the leaves at the tops of the trees.

What a relief to feel it hush over him too as it dipped from the heights to blow him down the path. What if he put his cape on and let it catch like a sail, he smiled. He could fly over everyone and nobody would know.

When the apartment building arrived, he bobbed up the steps, in the door, across the transom and weary, carpeted stairway that stacked to his third floor room.

Taped on the door was a cheese colored notice from the Ajax Furniture Company. Due to lack of payment, it said, they had stopped in to take back the sofa he was paying on.

"Agh!" Earl spluttered, fumbling with the keys, dropping letters, opening the lock at last.

The sofa's place by the window was too much green moonlight and empty space. They really did it, he grieved, but it wasn't the sofa that was such a loss—he kept treasure in one of its cushions. His big hope to get him out of all of this was his monster-movie script. He ran over to the flattened shape of carpet but there was nothing there.

Earl curled down in deflation on the scene of the crime and pushed himself to sleep. Sunlight was needed to save the remains.

***

In the early morning, Earl stood in the trolley station for half an hour, waiting for someone to throw away a trolley transfer. Finally it happened. A woman stepped off the #5 and tossed her ticket into the basket. It was stamped until 7:30, enough time to get him to Ajax. He would find his papers in the sofa and never have to go back there again after this ride.

Oh, it was always an adventure when he rode the trolley. Sitting down in front, he looked forward to something happening.

A man wearing a War Veteran hat was holding a plastic bag of peanuts. He was taking the nuts out and ordering them on his leg like a little television segment from the golden age.

Earl smiled, he needed this distraction.

With small, slow uttered words, the man said at last, "The glass tubes of Mars." That was it...Simple. Some burble from his past, who knows which war or shock leaked it, then, one by one, he plucked each nut and put them all back in the bag, signaled the driver to stop and was out hobbling at the next red light.

Now that Earl's short movie was over, all he had to watch was the shaky windows showing him the rundown state of the city. Each sorry roof ran into the next like crumbling waves of brick, pressboard, tin and plastic. The scratchy electric wire lines sloped off angles around the bent chimneys, TV antennas on roofs and steeples, wash laid out on the strings like signal flags in the wind. Yes, it was a long hard fall from those few years ago when things were different.

The numbered streets told him when it was time to leave. He pulled the bell-string and the trolley stopped at the next curb.

Even though he had a ticket, the driver still had to give him a hard time.

"Lemme see it," he said, taking his hands from the rudder to seize Earl's little strip of paper.

Earl had been through this before. Some of the drivers were this way, something about the job made them change into these heartless robots, no different than the enemy was supposed to be. "It's okay," Earl humored him, "it's good until 7.30," and he just left.

The Ajax Furniture Co. was a long lying-down warehouse. It leaned over the concrete a few yards from him. A fuzzy string of neon lights were already buzzing along the rain-gutter, and on the sidewalk before the doors, different kinds of chairs had been set out for sale, still so early that their claws held dew.

Earl went past the sounds of their price tags rattle, and there he was inside, in the middle of a show of aisles. It was like a factory. A loud forklift went by, carrying a pallet wrapped with rolls of remnant carpet.

Past a row of footstools—Earl was going by too fast to look at or care about—and his shadow led him around the corner to the sofas. He slowed down to examine them, their colors and cloths. Squinting his eyes, his head clocked back and forth and his breathing was heavy from the rush of the exertion of getting here so fast. *No, no, no,* he didn't see it anywhere, and around the next corner were tables, so no, it wasn't here. "Ohh…" he stopped at the wall in his sorrow.

"Can I help you?" an old man asked him.

"Something kind of sad happened, my sofa got repossessed. I have the money for it, I was going to pay, today or yesterday," he patted his empty pocket. "I want to buy it back, but I don't see it here."

The old man nodded the pulleys in his wiry neck. "Could be it's in the loading bay, or in the truck still."

"Where? Where's that?"

"Through here," he pointed at the No Admittance sign, "but I'll have to get the manager to let you in there. We have to—"

"Pah!" said Earl, slapping the thing open with his palm and entering. The sound had welled out of him, he had come this far, he couldn't stop, it meant the world to him.

"Hey! I'm getting the manager!"

Earl saw the truck backed up to the loading bay. Its roll door open, and packed in the gloom with stacked chairs and lamps and other furniture, Earl could see his sofa

"That's it!" Earl waddled across the long shadows and kerosene beams.

When he hopped onto the truck ramp, the dark metal cluttered hollow gave to his weight. He hurried to push aside a rocking chair that hit him as he leaned over to paw at the sofa's cushions.

Grabbing the middle pillow, he jerked the zipper on it loose and pulled out the white foam stuffing. The cardboard bound pages of his manuscript fell out of a cloud.

Earl let out a laugh as he pressed his book under his shirt and withdrew from the truck.

He looked around for an escape. Now that he needed to get out, he didn't know how. The truck filled the loading bay's doorway. He could see the narrow sunlight past its fit, but he couldn't slip through to safety outside.

They were coming for him any second. If he could just hide from sight while they came and went, he could find the door out in the quiet afterwards. He bounced back into the truck.

Behind a grandfather clock and a roll of maps, stood a tall Egyptian sarcophagus, a trick coffin from a magic show in debt, and he hurried himself, breaking the sealed edges, leaping into it and slamming the door.

Dark inside, he bumped into something yielding that sighed.

The terrifying thought of being trapped with a cursed mummy rushed in on him, but he couldn't move for fear. Someone was in there with him. He heard the sandy sound, hands rubbing together, faster, making friction, sparking a slow yellow glow. A woman's shape appeared from the dim, her neon form curving into view clearer than a heating television picture tube. She shed enough warmth to fill the chamber.

His thick weak heart fluttered and melted like a pat of butter.

***

The old man arrived pushing a hand-truck, followed by the manager and a man who wore a tuxedo cobwebbed together.

"It was purely my secretary's error," the sorry stage performer was telling them his apology. "We didn't realize our mistake until we added up all the weeks and found we counted wrong."

"Yeah, well calm down. You paid up Marconi, so you're okay for now," the manager replied. They stopped by the truck. "Les, will give you a hand. Get that coffin out of there, Les," he tapped the old man.

The old man ran the dolly under the sarcophagus and tipped it on. He heaved and staggered like a bending twig.

"Careful please," Marconi the Magician put his long bony frame against the oblong box to steady it.

"Yeah," said the manager dryly, adding, "It's his until next month when we take it back again."

Marconi steadied the mummy case, "Not this time! I expect to be booked on a major transcontinental tour. We'll be playing to the delight of audiences from coast to coast. In another month's time, I'll send you the sum total of what you're owed."

"Alright, settle, settle. So you've finally discovered talent. How fortunate. Maybe I'll go down to the theater and see how far this talent is going." The manager left them wrestling the sarcophagus over the splintered wooden loading dock. Deciding out loud, "I think I will," he went back through the doors to the store, cigar threading a linger behind him.

"Where you want this casket?" wheezed the old man at Marconi, as he wheeled it unsteadily, in degrees, bending knees.

"I borrowed a friend's carriage. It's in the lot."

They went out a side door creaked into the tier and timber of the shadowy wall. Sunlight broke on them, some seagulls ran away from them across the cracked tar.

"There," said Marconi, pointing to a lopsided war-surplus electrical cart. Its mottled army-green was rusting off in great rain splotched petals.

The old man tipped the sarcophagus on, and together they pushed it into the bed. It fit resting its carved feet off the end.

"Hope I don't see that again."

"You won't…" Marconi promised him. "Unless you are one of the crowned heads of Europe, or a Rajah in a courtly palace uphill from the Indian Ocean."

The old man wiped his face with a red handkerchief and mumbled his way back.

Marconi pulled the starter for the motor and crawled onto the rattling seat. The cart hummed off into the light morning traffic, wagons, bicycles, and people pushing flowers to sell.

***

Not long later, Marconi broke through a flock of chirping dancing girls to stand at the curtained backstage. The sarcophagus was waiting on its mark over the trap door. There was no sign of his assistant this morning, but in all the running around he prayed she was already in the coffin awaiting him, ready for her part. He fretted, always nervous before the act.

The drums rolled, the curtain began to wave aside, spotlights hit the stage and he flew himself out from the wings.

"Thank you very much!" He saw more faces than usual in the dim row of chairs—a good turnout for the first show of the day.

He gave them a spring of paper daisies out the end of his hollow magic wand. He followed that with the endless knotted red handkerchief from the sleeve of his coat, then in the silence he quickly got to the heart of his show.

Tapping the sarcophagus three times, the signal for his assistant inside, he stopped suddenly and confronted the audience, "No!" He held up his hand dramatically. "I'm not going to show you what is in this ancient wonder. It is not for our day and age…Could we even begin to comprehend this magic? Who among us can behold the dance of Salome's seven veils, how dare we set free the power of such beauty and love to enchant and work spells?"

There was noise in the crowd working its way forward. "Or perhaps…" he paused. A clarinet in the orchestra pit trilled like a snake charmer.

"Perhaps such a lesson is exactly what we need, in this tired, warring world of our own making…" and so he unlatched the Egyptian lid.

The coffin opened, it was dark as the reaches of space inside. *Where was she?* Marconi felt the crowd gasp at his back and then again as something stirred in the emptiness.

A cloud slowly poured out. It was the size of a sheep. Each motion of its swirl pulsed and pulled it through the air like a deep sea creature.

It brushed close past Marconi. He felt the hum of electrical energy driving it, coiling it upwards in the heat draft off the spotlit stage, towards the ceiling over the seats.

He could see a blue patch of sailors on their feet watching it. He saw the staring dancing girls bunching their feathers together along the edge of the curtain, while the cloud hovered to some certain destination. Marconi and everyone else waited, holding breath.

It crackled along the domed ceiling and stopped by the dimmed chandelier, staying long enough to dim it. Then the cloud moved onwards with the mind of a balloon in the current, gradually dropping to a tall narrow window. The window was open. It waited. Outside was a purple staggering garden of city roofs. It was another wartime blackout, but everything was where it should be.

We're All Friends

"Excuse me...Excuse me, Mr. Nitecap."

"Yeah...You, there."

The reporter elbowed herself some room in the crowd and started over. "Mr. Nitecap—"

He stopped her to say. "Please, call me Tony. We're all friends."

"Tony," she smiled. "I wanted to ask you about your new record, *Duets In G*."

"Shoot."

"Would you consider it a little strange. I mean, taking old recordings of Crosby, Sinatra and even Caruso and then you singing along with them. Let's be honest, doesn't that sort of make you a grave robber?"

A surprised cry swept the room from the audience.

Tony held his hands up to quiet everyone. "You're very perceptive," he told her, then suddenly dropped, "And no, it does not. If all the best singers are ghosts, then so be it. That's the way it is. They're my peers. So I'll sing with the ghosts."

Tony let that be the end. It was over. He waved to everyone and left them through a door behind the curtain.

"What a nut, huh Tony?" said the little man scurrying along beside him.

"Uhh," Tony grunted. "Charlie, someone's always got to take a jab at that record. Can't they tell I'm for real?"

"Sure. The fans can, Tony. The fans can feel it."

Tony stopped. "You're absolutely right. That's exactly why I shouldn't let people like her get to me." He started again and his chauffeur had to run to keep up with him. "Come on, let's get out of here. Take me for a drive, Charlie." When they got to it, he pumped open the door to the garage. "I need a nice long ride in the moonlight."

"Sure Tony. I know the score."

Before they quite reached the car, twenty feet to go, the loamy and familiar smell of smoke drifting towards them made Tony smile. "Is that you Bing?" he called and laughed.

The specter appeared with pipe in hand. "Hullo, Tony."

"Bing, it's good to see you!" Tony beamed. "I've been missing you! Where the blue of the night meets the gold of the day..." he crooned, delighted by the sight of his favorite ghost. "We're just going for a drive."

"Mind if I tag along?" Bing Crosby tapped some ash against his palm. It drifted from his gray hand like milkweed pollen.

"Sure, come on Bing, let's go. Let me get this door open for you." Tony opened the side of the black limousine. His chauffeur got into the front seat while Tony gave the ghost room in the back, then followed him in. "Drive!" he banged a flat hand on the window.

Soon Tony said, "Bing I was thinking about that song we did together for the new album. You know it's sitting there in the charts like a ripe apple. It's beautiful. And I was thinking how much fun I had with you, so why stop there?"

Smoothly, the car breezed past streetlamps, corner stores, the tall yellow windows of downtown. Tony talked about his plan for the next record. "Just you and me Bing, we can sing all your favorites."

The back of the limo had been filling with pipe clouds as Bing lit another wooden match and puffed. He listened and hummed along as his white eyes roamed out.

Soon, Tony couldn't make a window through the cloud to see if Bing was still there. He was in a thick restless cumulous.

Tony rapped on the glass, "Hey Charlie! Can you pull over?"

In ten seconds, Tony had the door open and all that cloud or ghost rushed out into the night. It disappeared over the black unrolling lawns. "Hah!" Tony laughed in recognition. "You found the golf course! I should have known! So long, Bing!" he yelled.

Tony closed the door on the haunted sight. He had no idea when or where Bing would reappear. Life and the afterlife were unpredictable. "Let's go, Charlie."

Tony was not alone though. When he turned up the sound of his new album, he sang along with friends. The sunroof rolled back, and he could watch for stars. He held his hands up to them at the end of the song. "You're out there somewhere too, Frank," he sighed in memory.

The car slowed again and stopped in a parking lot. Tony knew it well. "Charlie! You're the best!"

The window between them slid down and the chauffeur turned around. "I just figured, boss. You want me to go in and get you the usual?"

"Naw, Charlie. You stay put. Relax. I'll get it. You want anything?"

"I'm fine, boss."

"Okay, I'll be back." Tony stepped out into a fragrant apple blossom canopy. He took a deep breath of the patch of tall weed stalks bearing tin colored flowers. They swayed around and clapped together in the warm hushing breeze. An orange wash of electricity surrounded The Outrageous Taco.

Tony had his list of favorite things, this was near the top. His mouth was already watering as he walked towards it. On the wall inside was a framed photograph of himself, autographed personally, so he would never really have to leave.

He watched the way his expensive shoes bit into the pavement. He tapped the shape of his wallet in his slick coat pocket. In just a moment he was going in the door.

Usually there was a happy gang inside to welcome him, but tonight was a surprise. It resembled a bus station. People were fixed on the chairs or leaning on the pillars and against walls. They all gave him a thick look as he entered.

He walked towards the counter. So what was going on in here? He looked around some shoulders and saw the girl in uniform crying. She was trying to take someone's order. She was getting nowhere but further into a bad dream world where she couldn't move to stop what was happening. A line stood in front of her register but she was all alone.

Tony stopped at the edge of the counter. "Are you okay?" he caught her by the hand maybe a moment before she fell apart.

"Everyone left," she choked.

"Who?"

"The entire kitchen left me. This is my first night of work and look what happened!"

He smiled so she would know he was joining her cause. Then when Tony Nitecap grabbed the microphone off the counter, he launched into, "Good evening ladies and gentlemen," and the place became a show.

"Folks, I thank you for allowing me this rare privilege. Honestly, I was on my way home from a sold-out performance, and I ended up here instead for an encore. Can you blame me?" His teeth cut at their cheers, then he fixed his hands together like a prayer as he wheeled to look at the girl's nametag. "It seems we've all been called here together to help Doreen out of her troubles."

She became the star in an old movie theater.

"You know…It's not the end of the world. If we can forget why we came here and be happy with what we've got to look forward to, we can leave peacefully and happily. Would you like to hear a song before you go?"

The room became a new room. The applause was such a surprise Tony felt it hit him with the force of a bomb. But he was used to that.

He started singing "Stardust." It was a classic and everyone felt it. The glow gave Doreen enough time to shut down the store.

Tony waved them out of the room so smoothly it seemed like a famous show had been and gone. After all their clapping was over, when they were gone, the place was nearly silent.

Doreen was tired but more alive now. "I used to think you were a real heel," she told him, "but you're not."

"Hey, don't worry about it. In fact it's my pleasure. This is one of my favorite places. It's the least I can do to help you."

"Well, you saved me from disaster. I mean it, you're an out-of-the-blue-mister."

Tony laughed, not at her, or her honesty. He was remembering what it was like to be that way. "Everything will be okay tomorrow," he told her. "Listen, you feel like driving around? The night is young."

"I feel like Lana Turner when she was discovered at that soda fountain and turned into a star."

Tony nodded, "Yeah. It's a strange world."

"Things like that happen." She locked up The Outrageous Taco. The neon sign was left on. Under its cloud of moths, the limousine had been waiting. The engine started as soon as Charlie saw them.

Tony let her in the same door Bing Crosby had used.

"Look at this car!" she cried.

"I know, I know, it's what they gave me with the contract. Believe it or not, I'm kind of a simple guy. I just got lucky being born who I am." Tony tapped the window when they were settled for the ride. The car glided.

She said, "To think, I was going to take the bus home."

"Hah!" Tony laughed. "This is better. This is a night in the life of Tony Nitecap." He leaned and opened a latched cupboard. "You like cashews?"

"Sure," she smiled.

They watched the streetlights and scenes change. Tony finally said, "I had sort of a bad day today too. That press conference earlier. Jeeze! Calling me a grave robber! I don't need that. Hey, I'd like to show you how I throw away a bad day. Would you like that? "

She nodded.

"Charlie knows. He's stopping, we're already here. Come on out, I'll show you what I mean."

He opened the door for Doreen and she recognized where they were, north of town, where the aqueduct cut into the sandstone bluff and made a tunnel.

"It's a beautiful night," Tony said. "Here's how it works, you go to that end of the tunnel and I'll go to the other. Then I'll tell you how to be a winner."

"Okay," Doreen laughed. "If you say so." She watched Tony's ghostly silhouette walk towards the green glow of aqueduct water. On the opposite side of the rock, the aqueduct reappeared lit by the lanterns hanging off old telephone poles.

"*What is he going to do?*" she wondered, "*Fall in and swim past me?*" She followed the trail away from the parked limousine towards the cover of trees.

The night echoed the distant town, carried brushing in the leaves. She thought it was funny that Tony liked it up here too. Every once in a while she came up here and sat on the stones beside the water. That was in the daytime though, when there were birds and the ripe smell of flowers. *Nevermind*, she thought, *It's peaceful at night too.*

She got to the end of the tunnel and stood as close to the aqueduct curbing as she could, held the wet rail tightly and leaned far out to see back upstream. She could see small Tony on the other end, framed by a foggy circle of spotlight, waving his arms at her.

Whatever he was saying or singing was drowned out by the pouring water rushing into the city, but it didn't matter. She just kept waving back at him anyway, knowing exactly what he meant.

The Wonderful Stupid Man

His motto was *Change Your Luck With Teeleef.* It was written on the wall behind his desk and printed on the little cards he handed out. I have one in my pocket. Ted Teeleef is now in control of my future. That man who bursts a tan three-piece suit pushed me with a small tight hand out the door on my way to my debut.

Though it's May, it feels like October. The gray sky above town is dotted with more bubbles than usual. When people get tired of being here they get in one and go. I've come close to it myself. I can't say exactly what keeps me here. I guess it's just hope, believe it or not. Times are tough here but Teeleef has promised me luck.

As usual, my bicycle attracted the attention of some of the neighborhood children. No wonder. On either side of the front wheel are big metal bins covered with old chipped decals of ice cream cones and popsicles. I have never been bothered enough to paint over their history. The boys and girls see me and are wondering.

"I don't have any ice cream," I told them as I dropped down the last of the stairs, "but I can give you some ice." They aren't entirely disappointed. I unlatch the right side bin and open it up. A winter cloud puffs out. I have to keep my artwork cold. I reach my hand in beside *Trees In The Asylum Garden* and *The Portrait Of Dr. Gachet* to scrape some ice free.

They are happy with those slivers and shout away from me into their next game.

Teeleef gave me an address. All I have to do is follow Chestnut a few blocks south. Taking hold of the handlebars, I point the way. The sidewalk is covered with violet and white blossoms blown off the boughs overhead. The wheel in front of me cut a cold wind through the bright color, and the spokes, frame and chain sang with rusty parts. It's that chirping sound that never fails to call birds. They rustle in the weaving chestnut canopy. I don't know what my bicycle is telling them, but the finches and sparrows follow me four blocks until I slow at my destination. The birds hide when I stop. They go onto the ledges of houses, eaves, or any branches they can bunch into and disappear.

This is the place alright but I don't know why Teeleef sent me here. This is where I get discovered? It's a laundromat. The name painted on the glass is Krabat's Laundry.

Parking next to the big window, our reflection stuck like a crayon drawing over the sight of all the spinning machines inside.

A big fan in the wall turned metal petals slowly, and out poured that warm blanket smell of every laundromat ever known. So I went inside, holding Teeleef's card to show whoever was expecting me.

A woman was sitting reading a pile of travel brochures at the counter. I had to wait for her to tear herself away from the sight of the Tropics.

She gave me a glare.

"I brought this card." I pushed it across the counter to her. "Ted Teeleef sent me. I'm the artist."

With a grim look, she folded the yellow beaches and blue seas under her palm. "See that wall over there?"

I followed the arch of her eyebrows, I saw the lime colored wall with the hanger nails. "Ohh…" I said. "Should I put the pictures up now or—?"

"Sure." She opened her brochure again, she returned to a thousand miles away.

"Okay…" I left that noise to the traffic street breeze and approached my buzzing Freon-powered bicycle again. I

slipped the two frozen pictures carefully out of the storage bin
and carried them into the laundry.

Once they were set on the green wall, they shined like
emerald lantern windows. I walked back to her counter to take
a longer look. People passed in front with loads of clothes to
wash clean. "I don't know..." I said over my shoulder. Already
I could see the tears forming and dripping down the wall. "Seems
awful warm in here..."

She didn't say anything, but I heard her flip another page.

I turned around. "I guess I'll leave them now. I hope
someone likes them."

"Yeah," she said, looking up for a second. "And when
you come back, you can use that mop," she pointed at one in
the corner, "I don't want any customers to slip."

"Okay." That was it. No sense in watching my ice
pictures melt, I left the laundry and got back on the bicycle. It
tilted and creaked as I pedaled, gaining speed and the sound of
birds.

I cut around a yellow blooming rhododendron and ended
up in the alley rattling to the back lot of Food Giant. A wall of
old pallets buckled and towered ten feet tall.

I rode in where there was a gap and coasted over clover
to the propped open door of the supermarket.

Some cypress grew up to the broken line of tar, standing
around and waiting for a breeze to bend. Deliveries come and
go all day. A donkey with a cart half full of goods stands and
flits its tail. I took an apple and polished it on my vest. It's okay,
I work here. My studio is in the freezer.

The door let in to a dusty cardboard colored room with
boxes stacked to the ceiling. Following the linoleum to the green
locker cabinets, I opened one labeled Enrico Spumoni.

My fur coat hung with a pair of earmuffs, thin gloves
and a scarf. I put all that on over me and grabbed the little black
transistor radio to keep me company while I worked.

Dressed for the arctic with the antenna fed out towards
the KGUS wavelength, I unlatched the heavy silver clasp of the
freezer and walked in.

Over in the corner of my space, there are some ice-canvases leaning. I put the radio onto a twenty pound bag of peas and picked up an unfinished landscape. If I can finish this and another one, maybe Teeleef will have some home lined up for them tomorrow.

Just as I began to carve at the clouds the door opened and, "Hey Enrico!" a voice called me. "You got a phone call!"

Setting the picture back with the others, I left the frozen world. "Thanks, Oscar."

The phone was waiting on a box of pears. First I had to take off layers so I could adapt to the hot stockroom. Shaking the ice off my hands I picked up the receiver. "Hello, this is Enrico."

"Ted Teeleef. Did you get to Krabat's?"

"Yeah. I gave them two things. They're probably water by now."

"So what lasts?" cackled Teeleef.

"Well, why'd you send me to a laundry anyway? I'm not so sure about this anymore..."

"Listen," I could hear his tight grin, "You need to go through some hard times like everyone else does, some losses to see what you're made of, before you're there. It wouldn't be fair of me to set you on top of the world right away."

I held the phone in my cold hand, then switched it to the other ear.

"I've got an address for you. You got paper and pencil?"

I did. I said, "Sure." I wrote it down, the numbers and the name of a flower street. Maybe that was better, maybe not. "I guess I'll find out what it is tomorrow?" I asked.

Teeleef broke off a laugh. "Don't worry. Remember what I said, what it's all about, taking small steps. Be there in the morning with more of your ice, Enrico. I'll call you afterwards. Goodnight." He broke the connection.

Well...

It was all so easy for him to say. As if I should be happy waiting all the years it would take for my pictures to melt and turn into a river the world would notice. If I didn't already see it, if I couldn't already hear it rushing along from me, I'd still be stuck out there on the floor stocking shelves with raisins and cantaloupes and putting cans in pyramids. My visions see more than here and keep me from giving up. That's what I was thinking, putting my arms back into thick fur sleeves, when the door to the lot crashed open.

Oscar was leading the way. He pulled the handle of a big wooden wagon dragging in some huge square like marble. The blue shape of sunlight came through it.

I let my coat fall off and I stepped back from their noise.

It was a gigantic block of ice.

"Can you get the door?" Oscar crowed at me, nodding in the direction of the freezer.

"Yeah." Then I got a good look at the block passing me. Inside of it was a trapped black and white cow. It was as calm as standing in a meadow.

Oscar and the two other men struggled to get it into the freezer. They were lost to me in the veil of cold steam, though I heard them chuffing it further back in there, boxes falling and then the final drop of all that weight landing off the sled and shaking the floor.

"Whah?" I called into the ice-cave.

Oscar came out pulling the wagon with one hand, laughing. He wiped his forehead with his shirt sleeve.

I pointed, "What is that thing?"

"A cow."

"I know. Why?"

Oscar shrugged. He signed his initials on a clipboard so the two deliverymen could leave. Pressing out into the day's late sunlight, they left the door propped half awake. "There's not much room in there anymore. Sorry about your studio."

It was true. When I leaned in the doorway, there was a wall inside the freezer—a wall with a floating cow shadow. There was no way I could get around that to my pictures. I could hear the radio still playing a symphony dimly far away on the other side from me. I let the door close. I had to do something else with the start of evening. So I went outside.

I like the way day crumples. The sky had a beautiful pink orange glow with streaks of blue. The drifting bubbles like pollen somehow dodged around steeples and spires and weathervanes.

I stood in the yard and watched one of the bubbles that seemed a little low and lost. I wondered what the person inside was thinking. Were they trying to sleep? How long had they been inside floating how many miles in a trance?

I couldn't do that. I've thought about it, I've seen the advertisements and billboards a million times, everyone has. But it seems to me you'd have to be pretty desperate to zip yourself up in a bubble and fly away, hoping the wind would take you to your heart's desire.

I stopped pushing the bicycle along. The bubble was dropping. I parked against the pallets, into the lean and vines and I hurried around towards the belfry shapes of poplars. The bubble was going to hit.

It brushed over the wheezing silver and green sighing leaves and raked the branches on its way down. I started to run.

Making a lot of tree noise, it spun off and landed with a loud crump into an apple tree. The tree shook as it settled in its crown.

I caught up with the tree, I put a hand on a limb and a foot on a worn buckled fence and I climbed my way into the shaking foliage.

Getting myself into a crooking lodge where I could stand, I reached up and pressed my hands over the bubble. It had pearls of water on its skin. It was raining.

Somewhere on the bubble was a zipper. Whoever was inside may have flown a thousand miles to be here. The zipper had a silver ring attached and it opened easily with a pull.

The gas mixture within exhaled. Papers scattered out over me, maps and cartoon colors and then an owlish tired face appeared. It took a thick second, a moment so painted that it could hang inside a golden frame. We recognized each other. Only a little while ago she was in a laundromat.

She leaned forward, more brochures fell out of her bubble and her arms reached towards me, "You!"

"Yahh!" I yelped, lost my balance. Slipping backwards, I tried to catch a branch, missed and fell onto the ground while she seethed in the leaves.

"I've been saving for this bubble for twenty five years!" she raged.

Brochures rained on me.

"You ruined it! How am I supposed to fly out of here?!"

"I'm sorry," I murmured.

"What?!"

I stood up in the shadow. "I was passing by, I thought you were in trouble."

"*Now* I'm in trouble! Twenty-five years for nothing!" Her bubble was turning to slosh around her, she would have to return to the world the way it was. Unseen forces are always at work, on her and everyone else in this town.

I had to bow out of there. I left her in the hard arms of the apple tree, waving her fists at me like a crazy wilted flower bloom.

I turned the pages back to my bicycle. I slaked it off the pallet lean and started the rust song of pedaling wheels. It was dusk and the birds would follow me home to sleep.

THE WORRYWORT

I stopped the cab and let him in. It looked like he was carrying an egret, or a white umbrella that wouldn't close all the way.

"Thanks," he said.

"What's that you've got?" I asked him. I didn't feel like going until I knew. You can never be too careful, or too alert.

"It's an oxygen unit," he said. He set it on the seat beside him then he shut the door.

It was the weirdest looking thing, tubes and retracting bellows sticking out of it.

"I have to get this to my grandfather, he needs it."

"Well...okay." I started the cab. Nobody was coming, I had looked both ways. I eased out into the street. "Where's the old man live?"

The rider stretched and rubbed his sore arms. "The valley. On Van Lincoln. This unit is heavy! My back is killing me." He gave me a pitiful look, "I might need help getting it inside. I'd really appreciate it, pal."

"Uhhh..."

"There's an extra five in it for you."

"It's not that I don't mind helping you out, but—"

"Ten."

"There's no steep stairs? I'm not as young as I used to be."

"No, no stairs. I just need help getting it to his room. It will only take a minute."

"Ohhh…" I sighed. I stopped the cab while the yellow light changed to red. A bicycle crossed before us. It pulled two wagons full of firewood sticks. "Maybe they're getting ready for a big snowstorm?" I worried aloud. I peered through the plexi-glass at the gray colored sky. "What do you make of the weather?" I asked him.

"Man on the radio said to expect some snow showers."

"That's what I thought. I hope not though."

"Oh, I like the snow," the guy said. "What's winter without it?"

"Yeah, that's true." Jeeze, what a conversation! This guy was getting on my nerves, but I guess there was ten dollars in it for me. "Where on Van Lincoln are we going?"

"32 ½. He lives in a duplex. Well, it used to be a duplex, but he bought the whole house ten years ago. He got some money from the government. Enough to retire on, you might say."

I had to pay attention to the traffic, but sometimes I shot a look at him in the mirror. I didn't trust this situation one bit.

We passed a couple boarded up stores. The sidewalk was sparkling broken glass and litter. This part of town made me nervous. We still had ten blocks to go.

"The old man needs a new oxygen unit every week. This is the brand new model though. High quality technology…" He tapped the machine. "It's supposed to last two weeks."

I drove keeping silent. At the next stop light, I reached out the window and ran the thin aerial up the plastic siding of the cab. I cranked the transistor wheel and turned on the radio.

The voice confirmed my fears about the war and there was a 90 percent chance of snow.

I turned the channel to some music station. We listened to a song and some more before we crawled beside the curb next to 32 ½.

It was an old house that had been repaired and transformed many times over its life. Someone had started to scale it over with red tiles, but they must have run out of money or ambition before the job was finished. The bare hedge full of hydrangea branches covered some of the old wood.

The fellow leaped out of the back seat. "Give me a hand, pal. I'll pay you inside."

"Alright," I answered. I put as much sawdust into my voice as I could to show him how I felt about it. Then I got out and met him around the other side of the yellow and black checkered hood.

"Hold this a minute, pal," he told me as he passed the unit onto me. The thing was heavier than it looked. "Follow me. I'll unlock the door." He led me onto the walkway. The lawn was choppy looking. I could see my breath puffing out in clouds. The machine seemed to struggle in my arms.

"Here we go," my rider said, fumbling to put key in lock.

I stood by the door with the oxygen unit threatening to unfold wings out of my arms and fly off into the sky.

"Okay," he said and sprung the door. "This way… I'm here!" he called out to the house.

I couldn't see who he was talking to, a bellow was blocking my view, but I could hear a baby crying, a stereo and the smell of something good cooking in the kitchen. Footsteps patted up to greet us.

"You got a funny one, Uncle Bill."

"Top of the line," he told the girl, then pulled my left arm, "This way."

We went into a hallway and my shoes followed carpeting to the brilliant light of a room.

"Here, you can set that down," Bill told me, helping me at last to set the thing down beside the wall.

I straightened my back miserably.

"Yeah, it's heavy huh, pal. Try carrying that from the store on Eighth and Willow. Good thing you came along, pal."

I was staring around me. The little girl, not much younger than my daughter was staring at me.

Bill pushed the unit over to the wall and opened a cupboard sized door. While he pulled the tubes out of the old unit pushed in there, twisted knobs and fit the brand new one in place, I stood there waiting to get out of that room.

"My grandpa can't see," the girl told me.

"Oh yeah?" I started, but there was a sudden rush of air before the escape valve was tightened and Bill stood up again.

"There," he said, then he knocked gently on the wallpaper.

We all heard the reply and jumped a little.

"Who's out there?!"

"It's me, Bill, and Eleanor. And the cabbie who helped me carry in the new oxygen."

"Is it lunch time yet?" the muffled voice asked.

"Uhh, not quite."

"Well, why don't you keep it down and let me rest? What's the point of waking me up?"

"I...okay, Grandpa. We'll let you nap."

"Have good dreams!" the little girl sang out to the wall.

"Okay, darling."

Then a panel I thought was decoration popped open on a hinge and a pale tan hand came out to wave. After that, the fingers clawed the edge of the panel door and they pulled the shutter closed again.

"We can go now," Bill told me. I was ready. The girl ran ahead of us, out to the hall, all the way to the front door which she opened and stood beside, staring at me. Cold air pushed some dried brown leaves scuttling like crabs over the threshold.

Bill dug in his pocket and took out some folded dollars.

"So..." I pointed a thumb back down the hallway.

"Grandpa's been in there for, must be almost twenty years," he explained. "He was building a wall in that room and got stuck in the quick dry. There's nothing more we can do—to try and break him out of that would kill him. So..." he peeled off some money, careful not to give me more than he promised. "We try to keep him comfortable."

I nodded my head with empathy. "Right. I've heard of things like that."

"Sure. Happens all the time..." He passed me the fare and ten dollars more and I pulled it from his hand. "Appreciate the help," he said as I left.

"Alright." I looked at the cement sky. I rubbed my hands together. Tree branches scraped the sagging telephone wires. The snow must be less than half a day away.

I was grateful to get back in the cab. I ran up the green flag so people could hail me if need be and I steered a hundred and eighty degrees.

I picked up two more riders before noon, they weren't bad, just simple travelers who wanted back and forth, then at 17th, I turned and drove towards my daughter's school. After lunch, her class goes out to the playground and I like to drive by and check on her. We had kind of a bad goodbye this morning when I dropped her off. I had been worried about the snow that was on the way. While I tried to make her put on another jacket, she broke away from me, calling me a worrywart and running for the school house door. Anyway, that was hours ago and I was sure I saw a snowflake, the only one so far, but all it takes is one to start a storm. I took it easy on the roads in case ice was forming.

I was only a couple blocks away when I heard a strange noise coming from the back seat. A sort of chirping that was rapid and urgent. I took a quick look over my shoulder, but I didn't see anything. I had to pull over to figure it out. The noise was continuing. A wooden tram shook past my cab, then I leaped out and opened the passenger door behind mine.

I found the source under the chair. It was a smooth white egg-looking thing. I picked it up suspiciously, turned it in my hands. The chirping stopped. Of course, it had to be something belonging to Bill, some attachment to the oxygen unit that must have fallen off. I decided I better bring it back to him. I took it with me to the front seat and put it beside me while I drove.

Recess had transformed the school yard into a whirling game. I drove slowly past the chain link fence, searching for my daughter. At last I saw her over by the swings. She wasn't wearing her coat. That upset me. I nearly stopped the cab to race out there, but the egg thing started chirping again. I grabbed it and shook it until it stopped. What a pain, I had to get this back right away. If my daughter waited to catch a cold this was the time for it. I sped away from there and took the boulevard, the fastest route to Van Lincoln.

My radio came on just then with an urgent message, the chimed national anthem, the signal for everyone to stop what they were doing and listen. Obediently, I steered to the side of the road and cut the motor. For me and everyone, time stood still.

"This is your President," the radio announced. The dull voice twanged, "My fellow citizens, the sudden terror and suffering of our nation is significant and it only grows worse with time. I want you all to know that I am committed to a future of fear, determined to confront the world with war. We will accept no outcome but victory. May God bless our country and all those who kill the enemy."

The radio went off by itself. Beside the curbs all the silent cars started moving. The speakers on the streetlamps were quiet again. People were walking where they were going. The clockwork had been rewound.

Worse than the speech, which was typical for him, it had begun to snow.

The rest of the way to Van Lincoln was tense and I fought the roads beginning to slick over. I carefully braked, tested the grip of my tires and approached the familiar block where the house at 32 ½ belonged.

It wasn't there. Where the house had been was a weed growing lot.

I stopped the cab and got out. My shoes slid into the thin coat of white as I moved on the silent cold onto the sidewalk. There was still a path, but it faded into the weeds and fresh snow. No sign that a house had been on that lot.

I turned around when I heard the thing I left in the cab bleating again. The chirping became more rapid, then a steady beep, then my cab vanished.

I was standing in a war zone. Panicked, I turned and ran across the snow, what used to be the backyard of 32 ½. I didn't stop until I made it to the sidewalk on the other side of the block.

The snow was undisturbed, laid out like a muslin blanket over the whole neighborhood that only my scared footsteps had fallen across. I tried to let my breath adjust to the quiet world of the cold falling snow.

Flying People

When a person is dreaming, radar passes right through them. Even after discovering this, verifying it in one experiment after another, Irvam Nashteer wasn't sure what to do with this remarkable knowledge. He cut the power to the swiveling aerial, threw a black curtain over it and woke his snoring patient.

"Mr. Hursky, your session is over."

With a groan, Irvam's client rolled onto his back and stared at the ceiling, blinking, rubbing his eyes. He mumbled, "Thanks." Despite the treatment, it didn't take him long to start talking about cigarettes, but Irvam wasn't listening.

His eyes followed the stitching rise and fall of the swallows out over the parking lot. His distraction took him far enough away from his office to the most fantastic vision no radar could detect.

The telephone rang and interrupted his notebook diagrams. "Nashteer Hypnosis and Mentalist Therapies," he answered automatically.

"Irv! It's me, listen what are you up to tonight? Correction, I'll tell you what you're doing tonight. You're coming to my barbeque. I'll be watching for you, Irv. See you then."

Irvam was left holding an empty phone. He set it back on the cradle. That was his neighbor, Matt or Pat, or whatever his name was, with another attempt to make Irvam feel welcome. They seemed incapable of understanding.

It was twilight as the small electricar pulled into the red clay driveway and stopped. Sure enough, just across the street was aglow with checkered lights and loud mariachi music from the other side of the fence.

Irvam unfolded his car door and got out. For a second he wished could disappear into his dark house, but it just wasn't going to happen.

A sign popped out of the swaying thick leaves overhead and frazzled with the static image of the party waiting for him.

"Irv! It's about time!" The blurry dotted cartoon of his neighbor flapped at him. "Get over here, pal!" The sign redirected Irvam as he tried to move toward his house, it pushed against him, shining colors and bleating until he got the picture.

"Alright, alright..." Irvam sighed, "I'm on my way."

"That a boy, Irv!" The sign jostled and coasted on its wires back to its origin.

Irvam was tired of all this, but he knew it wouldn't last much longer. After he put his plan into action, everything would change and their rotten system would crumple and fall.

"Hey Irv!" The silhouette hung over the plastic fence, waving at him. "What took you so long? Burning the midnight oil?" And the dark shape broke into laughter, "Get on over here!"

Irvam swatted at the fireflies that circled him. Once he got into the street, under the stars and clear of the leaves, they disappeared.

His neighbor, Bill or Will, or whatever his name was, held the gate open for him. The mariachi spilled out too. That was the latest craze, they never held onto anything that lasted long. That's how it went with them.

"Good to see you, Irv. I've been waiting for you."

Irvam went in and got slapped on the back like an old friend arriving. The gate clacked behind him, the night already taken over by the barbeque.

"Come on over here, by the fire. This is the place to be." On a heap of split tinder, an entire deer was roasting, legs pointed up towards the stars. "Have a seat here. Let me get you a plate."

"Not much please," Irvam insisted, though he was quickly given a plateful of the meat. In the flickering light Irvam looked down at his feet; the red dust had stained his white pants.

Later that night, Irvam had assembled more than thirty people in a moonlit field. They were all sleeping, they were in his control. They stood in a tightly fit circle, arms and feet locked to each other, their bodies cast shadows like spokes inside a wheel. The quiet night wasn't terribly cold, but every time Irvam uttered a word it balled in an icy cloud that floated away from him on a current. Cloud by cloud his breath weaved a ring around the sleepers, then the whole thing began to spin. Irvam lifted the merry-go-round sight into the air. He pointed the slow wobbling higher and higher until it revolved a hundred feet above. At that height the puffing steam-driven blur caught the wind and ascended.

Irvam had worn himself out with their levitation. He collapsed onto a rock. He needed to catch his breath before he carried them further. The hoop had become distant and lost in the astronomy.

"Irvam."

He jumped. He felt a shift.

"Irvam, what was that?" The woman, whoever she was, came closer to him. "Remember me? We met at the party. I had to leave early."

If she was smart she should have started to run, right then, when Irvam was too weak to do anything, but she came near. She held a little net and carried in her other hand a glowing jar filled with orange and green fireflies. "I was collecting some electricity," she explained. "I saw a strange flying machine or something."

Irvam had to maintain contact with the air. By degrees though, he turned on the rock so he could face her. Yes, he remembered her from earlier. She was new here and lonely and innocent enough to be wandering around seeing things where she never should have been. He felt sorry for her and those who were like children, who just didn't know what was happening, but it was too late. Flying people were on the way. In another couple minutes they would float up there undetected, a few more layers leading in the sky. The next history would happen soon, as soon as she let him catch the breeze up there, but it didn't happen that way.

When she dropped the jar full of fireflies, that light, shock and sound of broken everything woke him right up.

All the Space It Took to Sleep Beside Her

I've been working on two stories for the pulps. That's how I make my living, writing for *Detective Underground, Shocking Space,* and all the rest of them you find on the newsstand. Imagination and wonder are the friends I rely on month after month, turning out these dreams. The only thing that has stopped me suddenly is reality.

Last night, my daughter and I rushed here, first to the hospital emergency room, then after all the tests, to a small room on the fourth floor, to rest. She has pneumonia. It nearly killed me to see her stuck with a needle, attached by a tube to a bag full of clear fluid, with oxygen running in her too, like a faint hurt creature come to this foreign world. All I can say is it ran into me too…what a world, what a world. Imagine where I would be without her?

As soon as she was out, into a dark sleep, they told me I would have to leave too. Visitor hours start tomorrow. I tried to show them all the space it took for me to sleep beside her, but they make the rules. Creatures from Saturn or further away…I had to leave.

Already though, I was planning. Once outside, with the sort of luck crucial to those phantom heroes you read about, I swam past the silvery grills of parked automobiles, into the shadows, held tightly to the building wall until at last I found the way up.

I'm as close to her as I can get. The ledge next to her window is about two feet wide. A paralyzed maple tree is hiding me. This late night is so without wind that those hand-sized leaves cover me from view. I can see inside past the curtain drop.

There she lies. There are machines monitoring her, surrounding her with blinking Christmas lights. In all her life I've never been this far away. I'll be as near as I'm allowed, I'll let her know I'm here if she wakes up, I'll tap on the window like Peter Pan. I can pull off my socks to do a puppet show…Careful not to lose a shoe.

The sky against my back holds a sliver of moon in the fog. No stars. The syrupy parking lot lamps, automobiles and the black gardens unroll across the ground like a crepe paper map. It's quiet. All this time lets me think. I have no idea what will happen next. The yellow green light spilling from the hospital glass shows me what I have written on scraps of paper.

Idea #1: Making Cake. That afternoon, Bench Francis baked two cakes. His glove sized hands were scarred, with swollen knuckles, from old fights in the alleys. He wore flour on them now.

There the story stops in time. I know he will make his two cakes. He will mail one of them to Sing Sing prison, while he and his wife will take the other cake to a party. He didn't want to go. He lurks by the big hi-fi stereo until the cake is cut into. All the laughter in the kitchen calls him in. He watches them pull the rest of a file and hammer out of the icing and crumbling dough. What can Bench do? He would think of his convict brother, tearing away at the other cake. I don't know how it continues, somehow it will go on.

I find the next tear of paper I started on.

Idea #2: Put It On Pluto. An industry on Earth sends unwanted pollution to far-off Pluto using a fantastic machine. Unfortunately, the machine works on the Archimedes Principle, which demands that whatever gets lost needs an equal amount to replace. There are huge container tanks in the factory, filling with whatever it's getting in return from Pluto. The containers tap and rattle late at night as the scared nightwatchman makes his rounds.

I can't do any more with either story.

Here I am, so tired, so terrified. I look in the window at my daughter and there's no such thing as fantasy. Whatever has got her doesn't want to let go. I crunch the paper back in the pocket of my shirt. There are bills, the cost never stops. I try to hold on to the bricks with her, as I fall into a forty foot sleep.

The Fence Painters

J.R. set the can of paint onto the ground beside the fence and dug a hand in his pocket. "Six dollars..." he held out the crumpled flower of bills, "plus change." Then, with all the bravado of a Hemingway hero, he told Tony the story. J.R's mother had given him ten dollars to go buy some white paint at the hardware store. "But I'm smarter than that," he explained. "I took myself down to Fetchits."

"Ohhh," Tony said coolly. Fetchits had just about anything you wanted but never quite the way you wanted it. A store on the corner three blocks away, it was filled inside with junk and there was more out in the cement yard in back where, when it rained, the things glimmered with the crust of rusted diamonds. Tony eyed the big dented can, all splattered with other colors: red, orange, lime green, and midnight blue pouring down one side.

"This was only three and a half dollars!" J.R. laughed.

"How do you know what color it is?"

J.R bent down and grabbed the can by its spindly rusty looped handle. "Look, it says White on the label." Someone had written that in black ink.

"Yeah, but—"

"C'mon, Tony! You worry too much."

"Well..."

J.R socked him gently on the arm, "Let's paint this fence. We'll get it over with then we can go to the arcade and spend the rest of the money." The way his eyes took on the light of the day, what could Tony say?

"Okay."

"First we need to open this can. I'll get a screwdriver from the garage. I'll be right back."

Tony watched him go. He stood there in the sunlight. Some crows scratched towards the park in the blue sky. He counted seven of them. Then he looked at the paint can. He still didn't trust it. The last time he went to Fetchits, he bought a compass that would only point its red little arrow at him, not at north. The Cupid-thing was always aiming at his heart no matter where he went. Who knew what color that paint would be?

J.R. returned, carrying paintbrushes and a screwdriver and singing like a cowboy. At the end of a yodel, he dropped beside the can.

Tony surveyed the fence while J.R dug the screwdriver into the enameled-over lid.

What a fence! Its boards went like warped piano keys tacked into the ground.

J.R. stopped humming to say, "Grab your brush pardner, I'm about to pop this."

They both felt the same way. There is that moment anyone knows when you open the shade on a new day expecting better weather.

What they looked at was gray. It was so concrete they could only stare at nowhere.

Tony didn't want to be the first to speak so he waited, wondering what would happen if he just broke from sight, ran off into the park, snapping limbs off cedars and hemlocks to disappear from here.

J.R. finally spoke, "It's almost white..."

That was the moment Tony lingered like a ghost overhead.

"We can fix it," J.R said next. "All we need is...something white to mix in...Flour? Will flour work?"

Tony got to his knees to look at the paint closely. The smell curled his toes in the rubber tips of his shoes. "Smells like something died in there." He stood up quickly and took a step backwards.

"Maybe there's still some white paint leftover in the garage. Help me look." J.R. led the way. They left the paint open to the world.

Tony could still smell the sharp metallic sting a few steps away.

J.R's sneakers slapped on the cement garage floor over to the back wall where under the window some cans of paint had been lined, ordered like a spice rack by J.R.'s mother.

Tony stood a step behind J.R. as he clawed hands over the collection. Each can was marked clearly in the woman's neat writing, "Red, charcoal, amber, yellow," J.R. read haltingly. "I don't see any white, Tony."

"I remember in school they told us white is all the colors combined," Tony tried helpfully.

"No," J.R. snapped, "that's wrong. What we need is something else that's white to mix in. What about flour? I know we could get some of that in the kitchen...Salt?"

"I don't think that would change the color though. Otherwise the ocean would be white."

J.R drummed his fingers on the shelf and looked round mechanically.

Tony said, "We could still go to the hardware store and get white paint. There's still enough change, we..."

"No. No, we just have to paint it gray." J.R took a deep breath. "I'll tell her..." he thought deeply for words, looked up at the sky, "I'll tell her it got cloudy when we painted. Come on."

They left the garage, returning to the crooked grin of wooden slat fencing. J.R. sounded more convinced as he said, "Everyone knows you can't paint white on a cloudy day. It dries gray." He shrugged and began to stir the paint with a long twig.

"You think your mom will buy that?"

"As much as I believe you've got an invisible cow tied to the end of that string over there."

Where the fence stopped in dandelions and briars, was the white twine Tony had knotted on. It strung straight out a couple feet off into the weeds.

What Tony saw leashed by the rope to the fence was his pet cow. She stared back at him with doleful brown eyes then nuzzled into the flowers and grass again.

"Ahahh!" J.R. laughed at his dipped brush that brought forth a thick burr of gray paint. It made a splat against the boards, spreading a rainy day as he drew it up and down. The fence wobbled a little with his fury.

Tony caught another lungful of the fumes and turned his mouth to breathe into his shirt shoulder, loading the brush. It made a ghost shape on the wood and spread like a sheet in the wind. "What kind of paint is this anyway?" he asked his friend. "It smells like poison."

"Fetchit told me it was used on the U.S.S Lincoln. That means it's waterproof too."

"I guess…"

It wasn't long before Tony was painting with one arm crooked over his face. He had slowed down some too. He stood back from the gleaming battleship hull and looked down the lean to where J.R was almost done at the other end. The cow crouched at the taught limit of the string with her head turned away. The fumes didn't seem to bother J.R., but Tony felt the world starting to swerve.

There were two fences now, a smiling gray row of teeth Tony lay down in front of. His face prickled with the grass, his hands held tight to the ground to keep himself from floating up and off into the open sky. Some birds swam into view overhead, performing fireworks with the blinking white stars. He groaned softly. When he closed his eyes it wasn't as bad.

"Hey Tony!"

J.R. looked like a statue was taking him over, he was splattered and spilled with gray paint. "You okay?"

From a foreign desert land, poured from a leather boot buried in the sand, came Tony's voice. "I don't feel so good."

"What happened?"

"The paint…Fumes."

J.R stood back up. "Well, don't move. I'll finish the fence."

"I'm not moving," Tony mumbled. But he let his eyes roll to the left where the cow had been tied. "Oh no..."

"What is it?"

"My cow."

"What?"

"Do you see my cow?" He lurched up on an elbow into what felt like a Martian atmosphere.

"Of course I don't see your cow!"

"I guess she must have chewed through the rope." His cow wasn't there, but she was never gone for long. He collapsed on his back. The world let out air like a balloon. The neighborhood was a kaleidoscope, a magic trick folding him up quick.

WATERING GARDEN

When the First World War ended, it was the war to end all wars, and city harbors were filled with steamships flying streamers, fanfares and bringing the soldiers home. People flew flags from their tall balconies and tossed confetti to the marching streets below. Then soldier uniforms vanished and started reappearing copper as heroic sad park statues, and people wanted all the guns to be melted down into farm plows. Newspapers wrote about the futility, the sickness of war with never-agains that were laid down like wreathes in Arlingtons all over America.

The house they walked to, that was swept into the corner of a dirt-covered dead-end street, had only one occupant. She wore clothes from the last century. The old woman used to watch them walking back from school, cutting across her lawn, and she'd always shriek at them as they crushed through her flower bed. They used to run from her, but later taunted her like she was tied up and dog harmless. They'd snap a flower and wave it at her blue porch screen. And she would howl and strain at them through the mesh and threaten to call parents and police.

For weeks now they had walked through her flowers, breaking paths through the petals and stems and she hadn't been there with her rage. They wondered what game she was playing.

On a dare from his friend, he ran up to a window and looked inside. There was dust in there, covering a frozen world. "Maybe she went to Chicago to visit her daughter?" or "She could be in a hospital next to a soldier with no arm!" They imagined her on a cot, guarding her flowers bottled upon the table next to her. Even in a hospital she would be mean and yelling constantly at wounded soldiers if they made any pained noise.

And so they skipped school and went by the toy store on the way to her house. Inside the front widow's bright red frame, rows and rows of tin soldiers were battling for sale with their field guns, trucks and biplanes and horses too. "We'll come back and get all of them with the money we take!" They pointed back and forth again to all the war toys they liked. It was sunny and they ran with their arms held out like fast wings.

When they got to her house, they landed in the garden kneeling and looked through the leaves and bright flowers to plan the best way to get inside. Bees going from bud to bud flew around them as they counted windows and doors and imagined Germans with guns patrolling the lawn.

The kitchen was the easiest way in, so they ran low across the lawn to that window, pushed it up and crawled inside.

Crouched under a wooden table, they listened to the quiet of the house. The walls were glowing wax-yellow and orange from the dry sunshine and the clock on the wall was stopped at 5:22. A wasp lay tightly curled up dead on the floor eight inches away. White curtains next to the window they came in were unsettling now with a little breeze. Birds were calling from the garden.

The only sound inside was their own breathing, scared. They motioned each other up and they walked across the kitchen like they were far behind enemy lines. There was a smell of something strange in the house.

"Where do you think she keeps her money?" They went upstairs. When the steps creaked, they froze to the wood for long seconds, listening, making sure, before moving on. "Must be in her bedroom..." Whispers were so big they could have got caught in barbed wire. They were so scared they were watching the wall paintings for eyes.

Inside the first room to the right, at the top of the stairs, everything had been gentled over in a coat of blue and gray dust, but that smell coming from somewhere was terrible and getting stronger as they walked. It had the presence of an angry ghost yet they left the room only after searching under the mattress. They had to breathe into their shirt sleeves it was becoming so bad. "Let's get out of here..." But instead, they went to the door where the smell clawed at them like yellow mustard gas.

It took them a while to process. Later on, when they were both in the middle of World War Two (one died holding to the beach of a jungle Pacific island) even when they had both seen far worse, they dreamed about that nightmare of a decomposing old woman, dead in her room, resting in the black chair next to the window. Her dead eyes were looking forever at her garden. Both their nightmares had her still alive though, somehow, watching them running and crying and breaking through her garden flowers for the last time ever, racing back to school.

Replanting

Though she sat there as quietly as a part of furniture, in the dark away from the stage, she was holding in her shadows much more than she appeared. She was holding the Costa Rican rainforest in a bag on the table. Reflected in the tipped mirror, clinging to the wall like a window against her back, I could see all the green trees inside as she reached a hand in. Hundreds of miles of branches and leaves in there with a mist coming from an early morning rain rising, evaporating with the smaller sounds of birds and insects and animals.

She covered the traces of a smile in her fingers before she closed the black leather purse, locking the golden latch. She had a plan, even though she sat there calmly watching the bar band perform hit songs from the 1960s and seemed six thousand miles away from the disappearing rain forests. In her expression, she smiled her own leaves of sanity and beauty.

After each song, she clapped a little into the crowd noise, being polite, and she would look around her as if there was a clock on the back wall of bricks that she needed to keep track of.

She seemed maybe nervous about something. There was a clock, but it was broken and its hands pointed forever at a two and a twelve. She had me starting to look at it too, but I noticed nothing unusual except that it was stopped.

It was only after the eighth song or so of her looking back that if finally occurred to me that she wasn't trying to see the time with her turning looks over her shoulder, she was trying to get my attention.

I tried not to start falling through all the possibilities, in case I found myself falling off the edge of the world again for her. I tried not to be suspicious, but her eyes kept moving me. Once I was going to say something but I decided it would be easier not to and then for the next long minutes I kept wishing that I had.

When she stood up, she held the bag tightly to her and her eyes moved across to me for a second, with the beginnings and endings of a smile. She walked with her arms carefully treasuring.

While she was heading straight for the door, I decided finally that I should leave too, twisting around people who appeared and disappeared in my pathway until I was out the door.

I saw her walking quickly down the sidewalk with her shadow streetlamped along the bluff of tall buildings. It's so quiet when there are no cars on the street, just her shoes making clicking sounds on the cement and airplanes spinning out of control above.

All the shadows were out on the streets, but I was surprised to see the stars out overhead. I was even experiencing one of those moments where I was picturing what the future could be. Then she stopped next to a chain link fence hiding the metal rusting bars of old construction.

Everything was calm now, the whole city was holding its breath.

Her shadow looked in jail and she almost gazeed to where I was across the street. Her arm went down as she put the bag against the pavement and daylight glowed over the sidewalk and street as she opened it up. The ground shook.

Turned out onto the cold cement, huge trees began to take root and grow up to eclipse all the buildings. And then, in the middle of all this green, there she was, across twenty feet of jungle, through a replanted Costa Rica.

CHEMISTRY

Across the dark pane of her window, rain was falling.

She turned on the windshield wipers and found somewhere quiet to park. She put out her cigarette, crushing it into the full ashtray and lay down along the seat. Rain on the roof and dogs barking somewhere in the valley below. While the black outside the glass would soon be returning to daylight, she pulled her overcoat tightly around herself. Her waitress nametag was poking into her skin so she unpinned it and tossed it up onto the dashboard. It bounced off onto the floor and she yawned and curled her legs up against the steering wheel.

Alarm clocks were ringing around town while she fell asleep, dreaming through a nightmare of tables, collecting plates and quarter tips.

From the factory smokestacks towering the center of town, fire and smoke mixed with the rain and fell inside water. People got wet running to their cars and fell asleep before they could turn their keys. Leaves disappeared off trees and birds fell out of the sky and broke on the ground.

While it rained and she slept, the rest of the town was turning into statues, and life was drowning under water. She turned over, with the sun on her face and hid herself deeper under her coat.

Now she was dreaming of someone she hadn't seen in years, like meeting a ghost. It made her wake up, startled, and she sat up to look out the window.

The rain had stopped, the ground was steaming and she looked at her reflection in the mirror. Her hair was turned in all directions like she had been asleep in the wind. She brushed through the tangles with her fingers and yawned awake with a stretch.

The park looked strange this afternoon. She had never seen so much steam. The swing set looked like it was on fire. While she drank from a paper carton of orange juice, she watched everything steam until finally the shimmer disappeared back into the sky.

Opening the car door, she slipped her feet into shoes, stood up outside and she straightened her dress and shirt.

There was a bird crumpled next to her foot. Its wings were folded underneath and spread on the tar, still as a drawing. She touched it with her shoe toe and it didn't move. Usually, there were hundreds of birds around the park singing to wake her up. They were all scattered on the lawn. She kneeled and took the bird into her hands. The wings against her palms started to move and it stood up suddenly, cupped inside her fingers. "Oh! You're alive. Just sleeping?" she asked and she set him on the sidewalk.

The bird flew over to the branch of a tree and watched her as she walked onto the grass, waking every bird she found with her hands.

EVERY FIVE SECONDS I THINK OF YOU

Lucy's first day at the sweatshop was filled with wonder.

All the people and machines, the river of cloth that moved loud on the assembly line and became stitched upon and shaped into dresses by all their hands.

These dresses are so beautiful, she thought, as she gazed and pulled at the rough dark blue of her own.

It felt to her that she was in the middle of something very important, to stand there with all the other women and girls among the clacking machines.

"Why aren't you in school?" her boss, Mr. Delisu asked, as he moved ahead of her, leading her to her spot on the assembly line.

"I was, but my family needs money," she answered and said again one of the things she had learned and knew, "We all have to work."

"Work is good for you." He stopped ahead of her and reached out a hand to a woman pulling thread through a guide. "Emily, how are you?" he smiled and held her shoulder for her answer.

"I'm fine, Mr. Delisu. Thank you."

"Good," he let her go and dropped his smile. "Come along, Lucy. Your spot is up here."

He introduced her to an older woman, Carol, who showed her how to pull the scrap cloth from the stitched designs. As they worked side by side, they couldn't talk, Lucy saved up her questions until the whistle let them stop to eat their food out of metal boxes brought from home.

"I've been here since I was your age," Carol told her.

Old lines etched her face. Her red hair was becoming gray. Lucy tried to imagine herself like this, but she was still a girl.

"No," Carol laughed, showed her teeth for a second. "This isn't exactly something I enjoy, but it's steady work. I've got children of my own you know and I work so they can eat and all. You're still young, you'll see." She smiled again and squeezed Lucy's soft small hand.

At the sound of the whistle, they went back to work with the waiting machines.

Lucy felt how it worked. You put your mind to rest when you did this work. Pull the scrap cloth off the moving dresses, become a part of that color passing in front of your eyes and blurring hands.

Mr. Delisu made the rounds and stopped against her small curved back.

Lucy looked up at his red face.

"You're doing good," he said and held her shoulder. Then he went on to someone else.

She caught the dagger flash from Carol's eyes, but she didn't know what it meant. She wanted to ask, but the dresses kept moving and she had to keep her hands going.

The flow becoming dresses passed her and she pulled away what didn't belong. She matched the machine.

"Lucy, you're catching on," Carol said once when the cloth slowed for a second. Then it all began again, for the rest of the day.

Again the whistle blew and this time it meant the day's end. The sunlight barely lingered in the tall, mesh covered windows.

Rows of women and girls got up from the machines and Lucy sighed with them.

"You'll get used to it," Carol smiled as the metal got quiet.

Lucy moved into the lines of them leaving the factory. Some of them were laughing about something and others were hurrying for the front door. She put on her wool hat. It was cold.

Someone pulled her out of the crowd. She turned and there was Mr. Delisu, holding onto her.

"Lucy," he said. "How did the first day go?"

"I don't know..." Everyone was walking around her out the door. Work tried to take her feelings away. "Tiring..."

"You're going home?"

"Yes." She felt out in the open.

"Let me give you a ride home." His arm went over her shoulders, gripping her tightly. "It's alright. Come along."

The doorway entered out onto a crowded street. Women and girls moved all around her. They had seen what he was leading her to, it was what they all knew. He guided her into an automobile. Autos were still new on the streets, strange machines that went along with the horses and slow traffic.

"Lucy. There's something I've got to tell you..." He shut the door.

She stared at him. The automobile sped and weaved around a couple stopped carts.

He bent close to her. "The company is bankrupt..."

Outside the window there was a booth selling things on the corner. She saw carpets and oil burning lamps, people all around.

She avoided his eyes while he spoke. She watched out the moving window with a hand on the glass.

Factories, spilled vegetables on the cobblestones, a horse, billboards, people walking in the street, pigeons and smoke.

"Please don't tell anyone though. No one else knows," he explained. "Soon there will be nothing."

Lucy was absorbed in the way everything was moving past them, all so strangely. This was her first time in an automobile. Nothing was pulling it, but they moved up the street electrically.

"Soon, people will have to be told they can't work in the factory anymore. Everything will be gone..."

Good, she thought. He's looking at the floor, not at me. She didn't like his eyes either.

"I have to let people go, they can't all work for me. Slowly though, I don't want them to worry. But I have to start somewhere."

He looked at her knees, then away to a place out the glass.

"I have to start with you, Lucy, but please don't tell them what I said. I can help you find a new job. I know people."

He was trying to be so sorry, she thought, watching the passing streets.

"There's nothing I can do about the factory. It's the whole country. Everything is in a bad time. But I thought I should start with someone new like you. You see I've got to let you go first."

The land was turning into the neighborhood she had grown up in. The automobile was bringing her back.

"That's okay," she said. *Make it go away.* "I can go somewhere else."

The grocery stand that went by was where she had to get cabbage for the family supper. *How does this machine stop?* she wondered.

She was very close to home now.

He put his hand on her shoulder. "You understand? It isn't my fault. I didn't want to do this."

Unlatching the silver handle, she got out of the automobile quickly, in front of the leaning tenement building. "I can get another job."

She ran to the stairway, jumping up the stones, and went inside, slamming the wooden door, not even listening to what he was trying to say to her from the motorcar. She felt she had to be strong and forget dark things.

Her mother met her and Lucy tried to act calmly, as if she had breezed through it all.

The first day at the dress factory, she told her mother, I liked it, but they just didn't need me. They have to let people go.

"They're going through tough times," she explained to her mother.

The sky of the city was black with the factory soot that clung through the night and made the moon look like a panther face.

Her two sisters were already gentle next to her, but she couldn't sleep. She stared out the window.

There were plenty of factories to work at. Her father told her she could try the shoemakers down the street. They needed people.

The tenement house was quiet, no echoes, almost everyone was asleep up and down all the floors.

Carol came to her spinning mind. Attached to the cloth, day after day…she didn't want to work for that long.

She turned over onto her side and pulled the blanket.

Only a few lucky days each month could she see stars out the window. Most of the time the clouds hid everything.

Maybe an owl flew past the glass, but she was already dreaming.

She was sitting beside a frozen river, watching. It was her job to pull all the floating ice from the river. Using a net with a long handle, she added to the small tower of blue ice next to her. Other people were on the other side of the cold river and women stood beside her along the gray bank. Working.

Someone was talking to her, her father. He was shaking her shoulder gently, waking her up.

"Lucy…" he was saying. "Be sure to get your pay for working yesterday. And try to get that job making shoes. They need people." He kissed her forehead. "I'll see you tonight."

She lay back down. He was leaving for work. Everyone had to, it was something never ending. The days were filled with it, but he had his hopes for something better too. There was talk that an automobile factory would be hiring. A man named Henry Ford wanted to build black automobiles by the hundreds here and fill the American roads with them.

When she returned to the factory the ribbon of cloth went along the assembly line, but she could see all the eyes following her. Lucy walked past the machines with the women and girls on either side of her. There was a long way to get to his buried office.

She felt embarrassed by the staring eyes. She watched the wooden floor go under her, the gray marks scratched across it by the feet of other workers.

Yesterday it was different. It was more than she could believe, more than she had ever seen before. Before that day took the wonder out of all the colors and sounds and different people, there was so much she didn't know. It was something to think about if you could ever stop working to think.

Lucy looked up and there was Carol, with her hands lifted off the assembly line. She let the scraps of linen push around her as the cloth floated by like rushing water. The whole old factory would soon be telling the story, how Lucy had turned it all down and walked away from him and his job.

When Lucy came out of the office, she was folding yesterday's coins into a handkerchief, returning to the doors, leaving the factory, departing like a glowing comet.

Better Weather

Someone in the kitchen, his wife or his child, was listening to a Western on the radio and spooning from a bowl. But he didn't step through the doorway to smile and talk, he wanted to get to the basement without being seen.

The door unlocked and shut softly behind him. Slinking his way down the stairs, he quietly tried to miss those bending boards that creaked.

There in the half light below was what he had been working on for so long. In the spring, before the war, he had started building, tying wires, soldering and pinning metal together. He stood there a moment by the tarp circle before he unrolled the canvas and felt the smooth surface.

His flying machine was finished. He flicked a button and the saucer hummed and glowed with a pulsating green light. Just after midnight tonight, he would take off from the field and soar in a wide returning circle.

"Daddy!" his daughter's voice called from upstairs. "Daddy!"

Quickly, he pulled the tarp back on the saucer and ran up the squeaking steps into the hall to the kitchen.

"Daddy, *Adventures in Rocket Space* is on any second!" she warned him. She put another spoonful of colorful cereal into her mouth and chewed.

"What are you making?" she asked and pointed to the door.

"I was working on a machine." He put the wrench on the table top. "It will make the weather change, it will make it rain." No one must know what I'm really doing, he thought, this has got to be kept a mystery from everybody. "It's top secret," he whispered.

The vision of a flying saucer, Martians, throwing out sparking lightning bolts on a helpless Earth army...Something like that...with creatures who dressed in silver and traveled millions of miles in their saucers...would be able to end all the armies on Earth. Only something from another planet could do that.

"You should make it so it can snow," she said and stared at the radio, the commercial for Goodyear tires. They were surrounded by green hills that got nothing but rain. It always rained, it hardly ever snowed.

"That's much harder to do though." He sat down at the table with her. "You would have to get the clouds to freeze. I don't know how you could do that."

"You could make a really big icebox," she explained. "Even taller than a skyscraper and you could make it on top of a mountain. When the clouds are coming, all of a sudden you open the door and catch them and keep them inside until they're frozen. Then when you let them out, they will snow." Heavy with white ice, clouds like cold sheep marching down the mountain.

She finished her cereal. The last of the milk made a little white circle in her spoon.

"Yes," he smiled, "that might work. That's one way you could do it."

The string of commercials ended. The radio became a rocket taking off, the fanfare began, the man announced with great feeling, *Adventures in Rocket Space!*

She played with her spoon like a rocket, whooshing it around.

The program flew around him; he was deep in other thoughts.

As soon as the show was over, as soon as his daughter and wife were asleep, he was going to go back downstairs. The night would be perfect for the flight of the saucer. The moon was a crescent white with all the stars.

Even if the thing wouldn't fly far and only tangled glowing in the weeds next to the highway, he would have made his point.

Someone, maybe a car or maybe a truck bringing lettuce to the food bank, would see it buzzing along fast, just above the trees, and think that the Earth was being watched by something more intelligent.

It would become a story told over and over, until everyone believes it and begins seeing things for themselves.

The rocket engines on the radio were landing the crew onto another planet, they were disappearing one by one into an unknown jungle. They fell into holes, into caves underground. That was the end of the show for that week, with them being held captive by bug-eyed creatures.

He pushed his chair away from the table and smiled at his daughter. "Another cliffhanger! Looks like we'll have to wait until next week to see what happens."

"They'll be okay," she said, allowing him to scoop her up in his arms. "It always works out in the end." Then she started singing along with the coffee commercial. "Good to the last drop!" on her way to go to sleep.

Before the news could come on, he turned the radio off. The war talk wasn't something that he wanted, it was death, bleak and not so far away.

Upstairs, he could hear his daughter and wife playing.

He got up from the table and took the bowl and spoon to the sink.

The water washed over his hands.

When night came and he reached over his sleeping wife to turn off the bed lamp, he would listen for a while to the quiet sounds of the country, crickets sawing like a radio broadcast from Mars. Then as softly as possible, he would lift her arm off his side and sneak downstairs, to the basement and carry the saucer into their backyard.

He smiled and went outside onto the porch. He could smell the sea and the rain creeping along the far hills. The wind pushed through the fir trees, swaying them. Everything seemed like the moment before the birth of the flying saucer, even the ocean seemed to splash up Venus.

The opening blue darkening sky was getting ready, empty for now except for a couple of clouds...

Benjamin Franklin must have seen clouds like these, he thought, the black kind with moving electricity in them.

THE RYOKAN READER

I live on the water. I've built a sort of a raft. I cut two barrels in half and lashed a few boards on top. Simple…That's what I sleep on. As a matter of fact, I woke only a short while ago. The sun starts me early. Away, thirty feet or so in the thickets of cattails, the blackbirds have been alarm clocking for me. After staring up at the blue beginning of day, I sit up, stretch and fold myself into meditation. When I have tuned my breathing to the world, I'm ready to begin.

There's not much on this raft with me. The barrel hollows hold what I need. Under a slat in one on the left is a wooden box I keep my manuscript in. That's *The Ryokan Reader* book I hope to get published, but if it doesn't happen, oh well, that's that. It's the time we live in, I know. In a hundred years, maybe then. Maybe not…Folded up next to it is my robe. I'll dress when I'm ready for land.

I take a deep breath and roll over into the lake. That moment is a lightning flash. I let it kill me. Then I have to force myself down and down to the bottom. For a minute, I keep my eyes open. Once the sediment has settled, I can be a part of the lake. There's a smooth stone I hold on my lap to keep me here. I don't need to breathe.

It's not unusual to see a fat salmon ponder close to me. Just out of reach, rainbow trout float with their porthole eyes watching me. What a stillness though. I can stay underwater for some time. I have learned to control the functions of this soul's body.

When I surface, the air brings me back to life in another world. I hold onto the rough cut corner of a Rainier Ale barrel. That is my morning ritual.

Now I'm ready to go ashore. There are things I need to do. I have to go into Seattle today. A seagull bats that way, barely moving its pearl wings.

I have a friend named Bill Everett, a policeman who drives along this part of the shore every morning. If he sees me, he'll stop. I don't have to wait long.

I hear him arriving. The black and white cruiser pulls onto the snapping gravel shoulder of the road and I reach for the silver metal door handle.

"Your holiness," Bill says, gesturing a hand off the steering wheel.

I laugh. You know there are people like him you need in this day to day reality. They bring to life what a bee knows, going to the same flower every day.

Even the car seat remembers me as I settle in to the springs. "How are you Bill?"

"Good. Good. Another day..." He sets the car rolling. He glances at the flat blue. "You going to the city?"

I pat my wooden box. "For more poems."

We go behind a pale gray sedan and follow it. The road takes the slow bending around Lake Washington.

Bill doesn't need to say much. We are just driving. There are people like him who you feel comfortable knowing they're in control. Think of those pictures of Franklin Roosevelt at the post office.

I tell Bill, "I'm thinking maybe I'll see a matinee."

"Oh yeah?"

Static crackles from the speaker. Sometimes I kid him about playing the radio instead. I know he likes Frank Sinatra. I bet he sings when he's alone on the road.

"I got today's paper for you if you want to see what's playing."

"Sure, Bill. Thanks."

He passes me the *Daily Times*. He has it rolled at his feet. When I unscroll it, I can't help sighing.

Hitler Asks Japan's Aid.

I skip over that. I don't live for that. I wish I could deny this war that I wish never happened. I never would have started it. And Japan of all places. It breaks my heart.

Oh, Betty Grable clings on the page I turn—the opposite of war is always there too. I can't afford her movie at the Liberty though. *Here's more sock entertainment! Double charged with more fun…Gags…Gals and laffs than you've ever seen in years!*

Bob Hope 'Caught in the Draft' is at the Music Box. I'm a big fan of Bob Hope. Funny, I've seen that film before…it's back again.

At the Capitol 'Shark Woman' is playing. *The strangest female creature man has ever known! Deep mysteries in an ocean full of terror!* Or else the Queen Anne is playing 'The Lady Eve.' I could see that again too.

Club Maynard has *Zandra*.

There's a lot to choose from.

Barnacle Bill at the Paramount…Or at the Neptune is *The Bad Man*. I'm tempted to go there. That's my favorite movie theatre. I love to sit there before the film begins when those holy stained glass lights glow. I should go there…

Bill is obviously trying not to laugh out loud. He isn't good at a poker face.

"What's the joke?" I finally have to ask.

He keeps it hid though, like keeping a dog under a carpet. It isn't easy for him.

"Nothing."

I try to give him the newspaper back, but he palms a hand off the wheel. "No, you keep it. Look at it later."

Something is up. "Thanks." I bend that newsprint into a square, set it on my wooden box and we keep getting closer to Seattle. You can tell by watching the gradual slash of trees and vines. Someday this will all be skyscrapers or maybe pagodas if we lose the war.

Bill's radio squawks a few more times before we get into the city. He lets it talk. Finally he coasts us to the curb on Montlake Boulevard.

"Alright," he says.

"Thanks Bill."

"My pleasure."

So I go out onto the cement walk carrying my box and the mysteriously funny newspaper. Bill leaves. He waves his arm out the window. He gets lost to me in traffic, cars and a bus and trucks.

I cross the street and go into the shadows of big maple trees and move along the lawns. The reason I'm here on the university campus is inside the wooden box. Professor Ume will fill it with more Ryokan that I can take home and translate. I pass a hedge full of roses, until the cherry trees branching out over the little trampled path take me to Eastern Hall.

When I say Hall, you shouldn't picture one of those brick and ivy covered affairs. Eastern Hall is a wooden pagoda. Green layers of Pacific Northwest moss clothe the roofs. It's been on campus since Ume helped build it way back when. The tomatoes growing up along the cedar shakes haven't ripened yet, they are still emerald green. Too bad, I could use one of them.

I step over the little arched bridge, wave at the orange koi below. If they weren't so colorful nobody would ever notice those phantoms in the black water.

A heavy padlock is attached to the door.

I stand there and stare at it. It doesn't turn into a bird and fly away. I know what has happened. I've heard it would come to this. Since the war started I've listened to the things people say on buses, the radio, in movie lines and markets. I hear about the relocation centers, I can't believe it, but what can I do? Still, I hoped there would be a note in the hiding place, where he would leave poems sometimes. With Ume gone, where will I find Ryokan? The stone Buddha in the ground cover holds an urn which can be opened. A fog colored slip of paper is planted inside.

Friend. They take me today. No poetry for a while—Ume

It takes me twenty minutes to get from there to the ship canal. I follow its pour to the shell house where the school stores its canoes. Old Duwamish is sitting on the stoop of the canoe house. He sees me coming and waves. He stands up tall.

"You going home?" he calls.

"Yes. Do you have time to take me that way?"

He points his lit cigarette at the canoe under the willow tree. "Sure. Come on."

So we go slow. Even if the world right now seems like it's falling apart and I'm not saying it isn't, I've seen the newsreels and I have terrible dreams, but I feel like I'm holding the calm of the world in this wooden box and I'm not going to drop it.

Old Duwamish was here long before they cut the locks from Lake Union and the salmon run dried out. He doesn't say much and I don't blame him. Everything is in our mind.

We get along good though.

I've made slow travel part of my life. Paddling into Union Bay, digging north for Sand Point, over the south end of the lake, I can see a flock of crows cross Mount Rainier. I look out across the blue water, at the green hills, the mountain rising in the distance. I know I couldn't be luckier to be alive now.

About twenty minutes or so, something occurs to me. I unfold the newspaper Bill gave me.

"Hey D, what's the day today?"

"Friday."

"I mean the year."

It's probably good I was up in the bow. I didn't have to see his expression anchored on me.

"1942."

"Oh great," I say.

"Time flies."

"You want to hear a funny story?"

Duwamish starts laughing already.

I turn to look at him over my shoulder. What a sight. He's laughing and I didn't even start my joke. The beads of lake water run off the paddle.

"What?" I said.

"I was thinking of Jack Benny."

He is still laughing. I can't compete with that. Forget my story. I look back at our green water.

Only in my head I think it's kind of odd. Bill Everett is a joker. He gave me a newspaper exactly one year old. He's been holding onto that gag for a full year! What a card. Today is July 31, 1942, not July 31, 1941. What a difference a year makes.

"Rochester…" Duwamish says, sending us along.

I don't wear a watch. I don't know how long it took, but the dot I saw worked its way into being my raft.

"Looks like you have a visitor."

"Yeahh."

A woman with long black hair sits there. She is wearing a blue bathing suit.

Duwamish gives a whistle as we near.

"I wonder who she is. I don't know her."

Duwamish starts another laugh.

"Jack Benny again?"

"Nooo…" he laughs.

I didn't expect this. As a matter of fact, she is beautiful to see. She leans forward on her bare knees and raises a hand to shade out the sun.

Behind me, three silver navy planes roar in a tight formation towards Sand Point. I watch them too. I am used to the loud thrum coming and going night and day.

When I turn back to her, she is focused on me with the thousand candle power of a lighthouse.

Duwamish is still chuckling as he takes hold of my raft.

She nods to me. "My name is Akari. Professor Ume sent me here."

"Ume?"

"He has a special assignment." She reaches over and takes a waterproof satchel from one of the barrels. "May I show you?"

There won't be much room with two people on board, but being close to her doesn't seem so bad.

"Well, go on," Duwamish gives me a push. "Three's a crowd."

I clamber onto the raft. Akari catches my arm as we tip. "Thanks." She makes me a little nervous though, elegant as she is. There's something about her that seems like one of those *Thrilling Amazing Monthly* cover girls. She lets go of me and runs her hand to the satchel again.

"Professor Ume needs you to translate this by tomorrow. He believes the work you do could affect the outcome of his sentencing."

"What? With poetry?"

"Yes," she says. "And he wants you to have this too." I watch the pearls of her bracelet click and turn as she reaches back into that treasure bag. And what she takes out makes my breath catch in my throat.

Old yellowed parchment. I know the swirled calligraphy on it from the years of making its meaning mine. It is writing like the scrolling watery surface of Lake Washington. "Ryokan…" I whisper.

"Yes." She holds the brittle wonder out to me. She puts it in my opened hands.

I close my eyes. I would try to speak but at that moment a P-38 pursuit aircraft comes roaring off Sand Point. I know birds and I know airplanes. I'll admit these things can disrupt meditation, but when I'm underwater or in the right state, they just don't matter to me.

Akari jerks her look at the sky and as she does so, her face becomes steely and grim.

I don't blame her really. They're loud, but soon gone. When it has blurred to nothing in the air, I drop my eyes to the lake. I can see the tiny point of Duwamish going gone. He was so quiet leaving, I got no chance to say goodbye or to thank him.

The Ryokan paper stirs on my hands. I hold it like a butterfly. "Is this for me?"

"Professor Ume says so."

"Well, I don't know what to say…I will do everything I can for him."

"You must take these to make poems tonight. Tomorrow morning I have to carry them."

It would be no different than any other night on the raft, translating by candlelight, only tonight Akari is here. I agree.

I'm not sure where to put Ryokan's calligraphy. Of all places most unlikely, I finally reach into the barrel near our feet and take out a comic book. My friend Leonard McKenzie gave it to me. He's young, he still reads these things. *The Sub-Mariner*, it's called. On the cover the hero is lifting a submarine and swinging a torpedo. I settle the ancient page into that newsprint, close the covers and replace it where it has been.

Akari smiles. She has to know I don't have much. What I do have is everything that matters to me.

"Akari. Behind you, in that barrel is my Japanese dictionary. I'll get my paper and pencil and we can begin."

So we work. That is, I do. She watches the sky and seems fascinated by the planes. When it is dusk, we bring out candles and light them around us. As the lake cools to blue, they give us our light. I pull out a blanket for her. She must be getting cold. The times that I do look away from the poems, she is next to me in the egg white of candles.

"You are almost done?" she says when I break from the page to notice the water is black around us. The lights of Seattle have dimmed for the war. In case a Zero happens to stray ashore, I guess.

"I'll be done by dawn," I tell her. While I write, I look up now and then to keep track of a spider making a web between the barrels.

I don't know how warm she is until she drifts a hand to rest on me. I leave my pencil on the word mountain and look at her candlelit face.

"Is it true you can hold your breath underwater like the fish?"

"Well, I can't live underwater, but I have trained my breathing. It's a monk's practice."

"Hmmm." Then she reaches back in her bag. "I read this newspaper about you." She takes out the article that had appeared in a *Seattle Daily Times* some lazy Sunday ago. It was one of those features they like to print on local characters. Not too flattering. I come off like some holy carny. It did manage a sentence to note I was a premier translator of the Zen poet Ryokan. "That's my life," I had told the pretty reporter. But would that sell papers?

"It says you can hold your breath for seven minutes."

I nod. "Sure. It's true. Actually, everything is connected. If you can—"

"Tell me, I wonder..." she leans closer, "Have you ever been hypnotized?"

"Hypnotized? Like on the stage? Like in the movies?" where, I thought, some poor sap was always getting led astray so easily.

We both look out at the darkness at the approach of another engine. She had me jumping at airplanes now too.

It isn't an airplane this time. I recognize the running lights of Leonard McKenzie's Chris Craft cleaving towards us.

"A boat!" Akari sits up surprised. "Police?" She looks ready to dive.

"No, no. It's my friend Leonard. He's just a kid. He's probably bringing me some food. He likes to look after me."

Her hand comes away from the edge of the raft. I notice a twine hanging off there leading into the water. Odd...She must have suspended something there. Maybe she's fishing.

Leonard gets here quickly. He slows the boat in time so he rides the wake in and I catch the sleek mahogany bow. The polished wood reflects our candle flames. We ride the last curl of wave. I tie his boat to us.

"You got company tonight?"

I put a hand on Akari's shoulder. It has grown ice cold. "This is Akari. This is my pal Leonard."

It's dark but she seems to wrap the shadows even tighter around her. From far on my raft, she murmurs acknowledgment.

"Listen," the boy continues, "I wanted to bring you this supper we had tonight. And also I wanted to tell you that I may not see you for a while." He passes me a basket from home, the slatted weave of it was pleasantly hot.

"Why not?"

"I'm joining the Navy tomorrow."

"What?" I ask, as Akari makes a hiss.

"Who knows," he jokes, "Maybe they'll station me at Sand Point."

"Leonard...I'm surprised."

"I just wanted you to know so you don't go looking for me, wondering. I..." he shoots a look at Akari who I guess looks pretty ominous after all. "I'll leave you now."

"You take care, Leonard," I tell him, taking the ropes off the cleats. I don't know what else to say. "Don't get yourself hurt, okay?"

I can't hear what he tells me over the sudden roar of his boat. When he pulls away, we hold on to the waves, before he whirls the boat and growls it back across the wide lake. I watch the white stern light twinkle away and blink out in the distance. I remember when he first started to see me here, he was only a kid then, not much older now.

She moves close to me again. The thick shadows fall off from her shoulders as she draws a bright necklace off her breasts and holds the chain up to me. "Have you ever looked at the sun?" Made of gold, it seems to grab every bit of candle, moon and starlight to sparkle. Her fingers turn it a little each way. Did I hear music too? There is a band shell on the other shore. Last week Cornelius Barter and his big band played there. This music though is slow and dreamy and maybe I am dreaming, maybe this whole thing is a dream.

Perfectly clear, I see a box, a little bigger than mine. It's green and trapped underwater. Inside of it is something so important. It needs to be retrieved. I can't fail. I have to lift it, I have to swim with it, I have to bring it to her. For the end of these dark times, the sun in my eyes commands me, do it for Ryokan.

The next thing I know, it is dawn and she is softly pressing me. "Wake up. Wake up."

"What?"

"It's time," she says.

Somehow I seem to know just what to do. I slip my legs out of our blanket. Yes, I notice the black dragon tattoo move on her hip as she stirs the blanket back. I'm sure these are all clues, but I'm no detective. I don't want to play Sam Spade. I just want to unravel those old words of snowy mountain paths. I let myself into the water. Treading, without a word, I take the white boat bumper from her. She must have taken it off Leonard's Chris Craft when nobody was looking.

"Go."

I paddle. A breeze crosses the water with me, arching little rills of fingerprints on the lake. Do I have to call back and ask where I am going? No, something tells me already, long ago it seems I knew. When I finally stop, I hold onto that bumper and wait. My legs pump lazily staying me.

It isn't a long wait either. Everything is happening on time. What began as a bee-like drone humming from the east becomes a yellow airplane, a Piper Cub, shining in blue-gray morning. I begin the breathing exercises I do before a descent.

It looks no bigger than a toy, then larger, I can see the pilot nestled in the cabin. Its bright yellow rippled reflection crosses the green, smooth water, over me, when a rifle shot rips a clank into the side of it. It falls like a bird off a tree. A terrible loud smash tears into the seamless cool lake. Before it sinks, disastered there like a photograph, I dive.

The sound under the water is of dry ice frying. I follow that shriek. It isn't far. The plane has crumpled into the arms of an underwater apple tree. Back in 1917 the lake level rose when water poured in from Lake Union and all kinds of things were disarrayed. I've found old cars, orchards, a house with a porch, and now there is a yellow airplane stuck in a tree.

I kick and pull myself over to the crash. It looks like a perfect catch in a wooden glove. Bubbles rise from the wing tips, the propeller stirs its last turn. With the clamshell doors popped open, for a second I think the pilot might have bailed out, but no. There he is, slumped forward in his seat. I grab the cool metal frame and look in. A bullet has pierced the pilot's neck, a thin stream of blood ribbons out and up. Behind the corpse, tied with straps onto the backseat, is my green box. It's the one I dreamed about last night.

I pull it loose. The ceiling of the airplane is pooling red. Akari urges me back. I can see her calling me. I have to give her this box. Everything depends on me. So I leave the dead airplane and swim back.

When I break the surface, I'm not more than two yards from the raft.

I see her throw herself in towards me and feel the water churn from her landing next to me.

"Do you have it?"

"Yes…" It's heavier than ever now. I'm glad to let her grab it so I can claw to the raft. I am coughing, water and air mixing inside of me.

But she is off, splashing away with the box.

I catch the raft. I can only hold on weakly. She is kicking away, almost to the shore. That's good. Ume will be okay.

I rest my face on the platform so I can catch my breath. There is a commotion in the sky, or maybe it's the sound of those powerful navy motorboats coming this way. I am so tired it doesn't matter. I can't move. All I can see is in front of me on the raft…the tumbled blanket and on top of it is something she left behind…It's a sniper rifle with scope. Her rein of wet rope ties the gun case to my raft. I'm starting to understand this thing. It's getting louder, nothing matters. My wooden box is cracked open so the poems are free to spill into the lake.

Medicine Creek

I don't have to worry about the factory. I can be away from work any number of days. I just show up once in a while to check in on things, make sure the line is running smoothly from assembly to the loading bay. The fellows on the floor give me the eye, like I'm the shark on the reef. That's okay, I say hello then I go. You wouldn't believe what I make.

I know it doesn't make a lot of sense to run away from that, but I just can't take it for long. Getting away helps me clear the wheels.

It was August 27th I took off, the Friday before the Labor Day weekend. I was looking at a five day break.

When I started the Ford that morning it could have been any other day, I didn't want it to look like the motor was taking me any further than to work. I slid into the traffic and pointed my way out.

I shouldn't try to explain the feeling doing this. I know the majority in this country go about the day watching the clock, only dreaming of what I do. I'm sorry, I'm lucky, I wish we could all feel this way.

I parked my car in the corner lot where all my adventures begin. I got out under the red leaf maple and walked to the window where the porky teenage parking attendant sat reading a magazine.

"Good morning," I said.

He grunted.

"Lot number seventeen," I told him as I set a short stack of dollars on the paint chipped ledge. "Here's five days payment."

He managed to tear his attention from *Heavy Metal Guitarist* long enough to grab the money and with his other plump hand ring it up and give me a receipt.

"Thanks." I still had ten minutes before the bus would arrive.

I knew how it would turn out. As usual, after a few days, I'd be missing that routine work-a-day world most of us live in. It always happens. That's okay though. These breaks I take recharge me. They give me back a little wonder and appreciation for life that the working grind would have driven out of me long ago. Like I said already, I'm lucky.

So at 8:15 I got on the bus with my backpack.

I sat down three seats behind the driver. Out the window was a cement wall painted with graffiti. I took out a book and stuffed my backpack under the seat in front of me. I don't carry a lot on these journeys. A couple changes of clothes, some food...I'm a free man, life is whatever I want.

It would be a five hour ride east, a new town I'd never seen before. Adventure, the way I wanted it. I flipped open the paperback cover and got lost in a crime story.

Most of the way there, I read my book. Sometimes I'd look up from the pages, the action, to take in the sights of the progressively smaller bus stations we'd pull into. An old lady sat down next to me after two hours, but I kept the conversation to a minimum. I returned to my book. After a while, I managed to sleep. For the last hour it was just me again and as we drove into Medicine Creek I folded the corner of page 343 and put the book back in my pack.

My first thought was: *What made me pick this town? There must have been a reason.* Sometimes I drop my finger randomly on the map. Sometimes I just like a name. I guess this time was one of those name things. Medicine Creek. Also, this town is a long way from home.

I thanked the driver and stepped out onto the cement. As I was the only one to get off, I saw the faces in the windows of the bus departing, watching me expressionless as fish.

Okay. Medicine Creek. I tried to tell myself the brick and wooden two story buildings held wonders. I spotted two gas stations. There was a Rexall drug store on the corner. A movie theatre with a marquee, and red crooked letters that said CLOSED. The bus station I stood in front of was an office tucked between a real estate business and a travel bureau. A big dusty poster of Mexico faded in their window. The last smell of the bus diesel slipped off the breeze, there wasn't another soul in sight.

Well, I've found that sometimes my adventure getaways run into a dead end wall like this. It's not that I was expecting Las Vegas, or Paris, but Medicine Creek looked about two weeks away from becoming a Wild West ghost town. And it occurred to me, where was the famed creek anyway? I decided at least I had to find that. I put my backpack on and tried a destination.

My feet made the only sound in town. Maybe there was a parade going on somewhere else, but the sound of a parade would carry here. I watched my reflection slide across the windows. It glided over the little scrunched man in the Watch Repair shop. I stopped.

I went back and opened the door. An off-key bell clacked against the wood.

He held minute twinkling gold colored wheels on his fingertips as he looked up at me. "May I help you?" his voice darted out.

Before I could speak, he rattled on, "You got a watch or clock that needs fixing? I also do radios."

"No. I just stopped in for directions."

"No charge for directions." He grinned his gray teeth. "What you looking for?"

"Well, I'm just visiting here. I was looking to see the creek this town is named for."

He let out a wheeze. His fingers trembled and I swore I could hear the tiniest clink of those cogworks hitting his desk, before he breathed out into another of his laughs. "Oh you're going to have trouble there."

I stood waiting for him to catch his breath and calm down. He didn't seem like the kind of guy who could fix clocks— right now it didn't look like he could hold onto a balloon. I rolled my eyes to the wall behind him, a shelf lined with sparkling clocks that looked fifty years old. I noticed the old fashioned phone on the wall, the wooden box kind with the crank on the side. I could have talked to Hubert Humphrey on that thing.

"Sorry mister. It's just that if you came here looking for Medicine Creek, you came here a little too late." He opened the drawer of his desk to look for something.

I took a step closer.

"Ahahh..." He carefully revealed a framed photo and passed it to me. "There's Medicine Creek as it used to be."

The postcard, *Greetings from Medicine Creek*, was printed in red letters across the top. Standing in a row like a fence of overalls and straw hats beside a stream were the corniest looking people holding up an enormous fish. It was one of those trick photography postcards. The fish was the size of a whale. It's an old gag, I've seen postcards just like it, with a potato on a railcar, or a bass draped in a boat, or a gigantic lobster. I handed the stale photo back to him.

But the clock man was serious. He explained, "The creek had magical properties." He put the treasured frame back in the desk drawer. "But," he sighed, "it dried up some time ago."

"How'd that happen?" Maybe I was finding something interesting about this burg after all.

He got conspiratorial as he resumed his slouch to cup his hands. "You don't want to know him...Doctor Hildegaard. The creek's gone and we all know it's because of him." He clucked and hissed through his teeth. As if that was all he had to say, he picked up his clock parts again and resumed his work quietly.

"Alright," I said. "Thanks."

The pathetic bell on the door clanked goodbye to me. A blue car passed by outside, driven by a blur.

Stopped there on the sidewalk I made a snap decision. I didn't want to stay in Medicine Creek, mystery or not. I was already thinking about my home, my record player and easy chair by the window. I could be there by evening if another bus was arriving soon. Goodbye Medicine Creek.

When I got back to the bus station, or should I say the door that led to a desk at the end of a narrow hallway, I cried out in elation at the scrawl in chalk on the board. There was a departure in twenty minutes! Had I only spent ten minutes here? Long enough. "I want a ticket on that next bus," I said.

I don't know what crypt they dug that embalmed ticket seller out of, he didn't even move as I reached into my jacket to get my wallet.

It wasn't in there. A panic wave hit and washed over me as I frantically checked everywhere. Gone! It got so bad I couldn't breathe. I rushed from the station looking for air. I threw my backpack down on the concrete and tore through it. I didn't have a cent on me. I steadied myself with a deep breath. Calmly, I let it out. I could see that old lady on the bus again. It had to have been her. When I fell asleep she must have got my wallet from my pocket. No difficulty there. Trusting fool that I had been, nodding to her stories of her grandchildren. She hadn't got much off me, but it was all I had and now I was stranded here. No, I told myself, standing up, I wasn't stranded, I would find the way. I could hitchhike. It may take a while, or I could be lucky and get a ride straight back home. Sure, it was all a part of the adventure. Nothing happened that wasn't written down already. I remembered the route the bus had taken from the highway. All I had to do was retrace it.

Sometimes I've thought of writing a book, a sort of traveler's guide, full of the dos and don't that I've learned on the road. This chapter wasn't finished though.

Three turns took me to the highway onramp. I stopped ten yards from the No Hitchhiking Beyond This Point sign and set up camp. That is, I dropped my backpack and sat resting against it. Hitchhiking is always whatever it wants to be, it's all up to fate.

I finished reading my book there. Occasionally I had to hold onto it with one hand while I hooked a thumb at a passing car. I also finished the sandwich in my backpack. That may have been a mistake—I didn't have much and I was losing hope. I don't know what time it was when I gave up.

I propped my book against the sign and put on my lighter backpack. It would be tough going back into town. I started for there anyway. I could call someone to send me money. I didn't expect to find a bank open at this hour. This would make an interesting chapter in the book, showing my human side and ultimately of course my resourcefulness when I got out.

I looked back at the car that passed me. It stopped on the onramp and someone leaped out to grab my book. It sped away, my book successful at hitching a ride at least.

A train whistle and low rain-like roll of wheels on tracks sounded from somewhere, and I pictured myself running alongside a freight car, throwing myself at an opened door.

There had to be a better way out of Medicine Creek. I would find it.

About five blocks later, wandering mindlessly, the way out found me.

I was on a residential street, I hadn't paid attention to the name. Large stately houses on big lots of lawns were spaced evenly on either side of the street. It was one of those picturesque old dreamy slices of Americana that Currier and Ives could have painted if there was a layer of snow. What was out of the ordinary was the rumbling semi truck with long silver trailer parked at the curb. Two men were trying to lead an obstinate black and white cow down the ramp. The rope to her was taut enough to walk on, a brass bell on her neck clanked hollowly.

Those guys were getting nowhere pulling her. I strolled over thinking I could help. What did I have to lose?

"Can I give you a hand?"

They let the rope go slack. The cow rolled her shiny eyes towards me.

"Sure you can help," the guy with the baseball cap told me. "Took us five minutes to get her this far."

"She ain't budging," his partner said. He flexed his raw hands open and closed. "Stubborn mule..."

"I have an idea," I said. I did too. It came suddenly. Maybe the cow read my mind and told me. I stopped at the ramp and dug into my coat pocket for my emergency ration. The last of my food was a crackly bag of potato chips. I took them out and slung the bag back on. There were six eyes staring at me in various degrees of wonder. I popped the bag open and pinched out a chip. Stepping past them, I held my hand out to the cow, close to her muzzle. "Here you go..."

She opened her mouth and took one step.

"Easy," Baseball Cap said. He and his friend hopped off the ramp onto the grass beside the curb, feeding out the rope.

The cow steamed along after me, her hooves clattering on the ramp.

"Easy, easy," Baseball Cap repeated.

"Where are we going?" I asked him. I took a backwards step up onto the sidewalk.

"That house there." He pointed at the white one with the screen porch running across the front.

"House?"

"Yeah, the backyard...You're doing great, don't stop. We got her moving."

We all hurried over the lawn along the path beside the windows and rhododendrons and leaning black-eyed susans.

"This way...This way..."

Baseball Cap's partner dashed ahead of us and opened the ornate gate to the backyard. A beautiful garden was hidden there, roses and topiaries and a statue of Venus.

Once we were all in and the gate shut, I let the cow have the chips. "There you are," I said. She lapped at my hand.

"You sure know how to move a cow," Baseball Cap shook his head and grinned. "Potato chips!"

"Yeah," I said.

Behind us, the back door of the big house creaked open, rusty hinges crying. "Wonderful!" said the old man standing in the doorway. He stepped out into the sunlight. He wore a long white lab coat, it billowed as he stood there, birch leaves rattling too. "Now," he said, mumbling down the three steps into the grass, "If you could be so good as to lead the animal into the basement." He flourished an arm at the cellar door slanted against his home's yellow shingles.

"Down there?"

"Yes, yes." The old man stopped beside it and we could plainly hear his back cracking as he bent to grasp the door handle. "Ahhh," he groaned, "If one of you young men could lend your assistance."

Baseball Cap held onto the cow's rope, his chubby friend sloughed through the tall grass to help.

"You really want the cow down there?"

"Yes." The old man straightened. "There's a light switch just inside."

The delivery man submerged then reappeared in a moment. "Wow! It's bigger than I thought!"

"Oh yes. There's plenty of room down there."

I felt the rope snap a little near me. "Can you get that cow down those stairs?"

"I'll try." It turned out I didn't even need potato chips this time. I had won her trust. She would have followed me to the moon. I led the cow down the wide stairs.

We were walking echoes on an old marble floor. Here and there were puddles, a little dark stream ran along the shadows at the far end of the room. Carved Greek temple pillars held the roof from falling down on us. The light came from Victorian looking lamps strung from the ceiling. In the center of the room decorated by a ring of ornate blue tiles was a fountain pool. A trickle of water burbled a couple feet up from its placid surface.

"What is this place?" I asked the old man.

"The Medicine Creek Spa."

"You're Doctor Hildegaard?"

He smiled.

"That's Medicine Creek?" I pointed at the shabby crawling thing over in the dark by the wall.

"Why don't you bring the cow to the fountain," he told me.

"What do you need her for?" I asked, but Baseball Cap was already pulling the rope in that direction. I guess I had tamed her for she clopped along. He ran the rope through a stanchion attached to the fountain. "This okay?"

"That's perfect," Hildegaard said. "Now, ring that bell there." I hadn't noticed it until now, I guess, a small bell suspended from the ceiling on a thin chain. I flicked it and returned to our little group. We all stood there listening to the silver ring of it fade. The sound seemed to move through us like a radio wave, traveling off into the ground. We held onto the last disappearing dot of it then another sound took its place.

A rumbling shook beneath our feet. The lanterns swayed. The shadows from Medicine Creek reached for us. At first I thought an enormous pipe below us had been unblocked, a whooshing roar of water moved and erupted from the fountain in the form of an enormous tentacle. I could hear Baseball Cap and his pal screaming, I saw them lurch into retreat from the room, but I stood where I was, sprayed by water, transformed into a statue. I watched as the tentacle swept its curling weight around the cow, wrapped about it and quickly yanked it into the pool. The rope snapped and whipped in afterwards.

I listened to the same rush of water rumble the marble floor. I wiped my face with my sleeve and stared at Hildegaard.

He chuckled softly. Maybe I did look like a fool to him. I still couldn't say anything.

He seemed to appreciate that though. "I trust you won't say anything about this. Not that anyone would believe you anyway." He chuckled again. "I doubt those other two will be believed if they talk. In fact," he said, reaching into his pocket, "I don't think they'll return for their pay." He took out his wallet and thumbed some money out, pausing as he passed me the cash. "You strike me as a sensible quiet type."

I nodded. I took the money. That was the answer to my prayer, right? I shook his cold hand and I left that house with Medicine Creek in its basement. Dusk was settling in the garden. There was no sign of the truck out front. The street was dead quiet and loaded with shadows. I patted the bills into my jacket pocket. I could get my bus ticket. I was on my way. I tried not to think of that cow, but I couldn't help it. Somewhere under this town it was roving all over.

THE RIVER SHOES

He couldn't believe there was a great pair of shoes just sitting there beside the rail. He stopped walking. The cars and a bus rushed by. Could they have fallen off of a truck and landed perfectly like this just for him? It only took a glance at his own shoes to know what to do. He loosened the gnarled laces his feet were battered into and stood in his socks. With a sudden loathing, he tossed the old shoes over the railing and watched them turn slowly together like dead brown birds falling. Funny how long it took, then they hit the river with barely a white of splash. Gone…Having an active imagination, he saw the shoes being plucked from the river in tomorrow's dawn, the police wondering where the body was. He was still smiling as he slid into the new shoes.

Instantly he felt changed. He walked the rest of the way across the bridge lighter than air.

Where am I going? That thought came as a surprise as he reached the other side. His feet had lulled him into such a peaceful state, his mind had been on nothing it seemed, watching the sky, the roofs and dots of birds. *Work!* He remembered, *I have to go to work!* It was where everyone was rushing to at this hour, the whole city feeding on the rush of people pouring in. But each step he took was taking him away from the café where he worked.

Three blocks later, he stopped himself again. "Work!" he cried aloud like a lunatic. He walked purposefully until he could see the café across the street. The sight of it must have jarred him awake. His sweet dream of walking rested while he stood waiting at the curb for the traffic light to change. Even just standing though, he let himself sink into his shoes. Someone jostled past him, a woman with a baby carriage, he had to move. He followed her across the street. The café was there, he had to keep it in sight, he was fighting it. *Work, work, work,* he told himself with each step. He saw the alley and the green painted side door. It led into the kitchen where the sink was, where breakfast dishes, pots and pans would be waiting for him to clean.

Oh, but he was still walking. He went right past the door. He must have shouted something again. He heard the screen door bang open, the punk music playing, the cook yelling his name.

"I can't stop!" he called over his back.

"Get back here! You're late!"

"I can't! I can't!" he yelled back and turned his head so he didn't have to see the cook, so he could see in front of him instead, the infinite and wonderful world that awaited walking.

He saw the whole city as a living museum. He went back and forth, up and down streets and alleys and neighborhood. He wore the day away.

Then it was night. His mind tipped like a failing wooden top, he could only try to catch at a thought and hold onto it like a moth. But somehow he had brought himself back, or maybe it was the shoes. He didn't know. He couldn't even think it through. He stood on the bridge a tattered wreck, his body had never ached so, his trembling arms reached up and grasped the railing. He was able to realize where he had ended up and it was over. He climbed up, slid out of his shoes and tossed himself off the bridge. The shoes, still good as new, waited side by side.

No Scavenging

The posted No Scavenging signs didn't apply to Bruno
Tarkovsky. Over on the south east corner, where the dump
was lorded over by the vast white pyramid of Mt. Baker, he
worked on a scaffold made of pallets and snapped lumber. He
found some good things, not every day, but his excavations into
what people threw away often uncovered treasures. This might
not be one of those days though. Dusk was coming soon, the
mountain and the sky were painted by the falling sun. Bruno
held a candlestick with the hook of his right arm and backed out
of the pile of garbage. Back on the packed dirt ground zig-zagged
over by tractor tracks, he stood up and cracked his back straight.
He was tall, well over six feet, nearly seven. He picked a broken
vine of blackberry off his blue overalls. A pair of seagulls took
off from the center of the dump going back to the ocean for the
night. The only other life was a deer stopped where meadow
turned into garbage, watching him. Things were quieting down.
The last cars had left an hour ago.

Bruno had worked at the dump for thirty years. Now he
lived here, in a little trailer on the north side. He plodded that
way, past three yellow tractors parked in a row. An acrid gasoline
smell surrounded them, their still hot engines ticked.

Two apple trees, one on either side of Bruno's trailer,
grew out of big black truck tires. The apples weren't quiet ripe
yet. He examined one and twisted it like a lightbulb, a blush of
red on its yellow skin. He licked his lips. Next month he would
be making apple sauce.

He set the candlestick next to his door and went inside his little house.

Four hours later, he woke up in bed. Car lights slanted across his ceiling as the engine rumbled by.

Sometimes at night Bruno had to chase people out of the dump. Teenagers liked to dare each other there. It could also be somebody scavenging for copper wire or something valuable they spotted in daylight. Bruno heaved himself up. He didn't turn on the little lamp, but dressed in the dark. On his way out, he grabbed a flashlight with his hook.

It wasn't raining but a skein of water floated in the air, a mist that shrouded every shape in the junkyard. He could see the red taillights of their car parked at the drop off. This is what they pay me for, Bruno reminded himself. This is why I get my own house here. With his flesh hand he fumbled for the top button of his coat. It was cold. His skin was slicked with the brushed rain.

The car was just up ahead. He hated to do it. The headlights weren't on but the red brake lights were stomped on. The driver was in there, sitting, waiting to go, while two other shadows moved something big over the hump into the garbage pit. It dropped in, before Bruno got there, with a crash.

If he could have stretched his arm out, long enough, if only he could have plucked those distant figures up with his hook and flicked them off into the dark. They were going to get away. He walked faster but it was too late, he saw them get into the car.

A plume of exhaust smudged the taillights, the reverse gear clunked.

Bruno stepped off to a pile of pallets and watched the car thunder away. They didn't even see him. They hit a few potholes where the chassis ground out, but they were suddenly gone into the night. With a sigh, Bruno clicked on his flashlight and walked over to see what they dumped off.

It wasn't unusual to walk in on an event like this. It happened now and then. He wiped the rain off his face and got the high powered beam to paw over the junk pile they left. Deep jagged shadows jumped everywhere.

A couple months ago something like this had occurred. A car had snuck in, but he caught the guy just a little further on—a thin fellow in a black suit, skin so white in the flashlight. Bruno grabbed him by the broomstick arm. "I'm so sorry!" the man had wailed, genuinely. "I'm a magician," he explained. He was getting rid of his act at midnight. He wanted done with it. He wanted to go respectable. "I'm going to marry a good girl and sell insurance."

Bruno let him go. Why not? He had a heart. A few of the magician's things Bruno kept. More treasures for his trailer, magic tricks he couldn't get to work.

When Bruno got to the edge, standing in the crumble the tires had tread, he peered over with his light.

It was pretty obvious.

A gray sofa was the latest addition to the city dump. It wouldn't be the last one. It had an ordinary upholstery, simple looking, maybe bought secondhand somewhere. But the three D batteries in Bruno's flashlight had hit on one unmistakable sight, a human hand almost apologetically tucked in the corner cushion.

The round eye of the beam sat on it for a while. The hand was a flower that couldn't grow anymore. He held the light on it long enough to attract a moth. Bruno knew he had to do something. It was a cold night, he was wet, he would have to climb down the hill of trash and get that body out of there.

Pagoda

It seemed to be a very small planet she was on. Looking out of the window, she could see where the edges curved on the green black horizon, where the synthetic rain clouds were piled up. Surrounded by seas of green leaves and ripe berries, the pagoda stood in perfect calm between the thorns, as a kind of blackberry lighthouse.

She had no idea how she got to this place, she may have come through a dream. All she knew for sure was the time since waking up. Sometimes, flashes came of how she used to be and she could almost remember other things if she wanted to. If she tried hard enough, small moments in time would appear to her and blink like fireflies. Through some magic she couldn't understand, she was here now, in this self-contained world of blackberries.

She had built the pagoda long ago: a Japanese thing of dragon beauty, with green tiles and dark red wood, tiers moving perfectly calm to a height of thirty feet. The rooms inside were quiet, with paper walls and furniture made out of wicker.

To survive, she had learned to make everything she needed from the vines, leaves and fruit that she cleared. It was a daily ritual, clearing the forever shifting and growing forest around the pagoda and all the moving twined pathways inside the jungle. After she was finished gardening, around midday, she would return to the pagoda.

She was sitting at the loom upstairs, making a blanket in a room lit by blue candles, when a shooting star fell. It went down slowly, rattling the pagoda as orange flame settled it into the courtyard. It was not like the sparking meteors that sometimes crashed far away in the fields. Something was different about it, it was really something else.

When the fire went out and the noise stopped, she left the window and went down the spiral stairs. For a moment she hung in the doorway and stared out at the strange gleaming shape. It was something she might have seen before, a long time ago, something connected to the dreams she had.

A door made itself open from the curved side and what came out wasn't that different in shape from herself. It wasn't wearing her blue and red clothes—it was dressed in the same color as his spaceship. Silver.

Things had started to change suddenly, like seeing things through smashed glass, or quickly melting ice, she was staring at remembering.

She understood him when he said, "Good afternoon, Captain Franz!" In that language she had forgotten until now.

She could read the letters on the spaceship. U.S.A.

She had a name too. She remembered Isabella Franz and things like photographs were shuffling.

"Looks like you've got quite a crop going," he told her. Then he laughed, "And I like what you did to the escape ship." He pointed at the pagoda. "I almost didn't recognize it. You've really made yourself at home here."

Isabella sat down on a creaking wicker chair. The rocket had burned the air. It was no longer the sweet blackberry smell.

She remembered how it had begun. It was years earlier when she was Captain Isabella Franz, walking across this barren moon, so long ago, planting it with blackberry seeds. Hundreds of moons had been converted, getting atmospheres, rich soils and crops, turning into farms for the needs of a crowded home planet. And this was one of them. This was a blackberry moon she had turned into a garden for Earth.

He was holding a clipboard. "I'd like to take a look at the crop before I call the harvesters down." She watched him walk over to the wall and he fed berries into a computer. A paper with calculations rolled out from the machine a moment later. Everything about the blackberries was broken down into numbers.

He smiled, "I'll go radio the farming ships. They're in orbit on the other side." He pointed at the sky. "They're just waiting for the signal. We can have the surface harvested and burned back in less than a day. Then it's back to Earth."

She remembered the sugarcane moon. Fire machines had scorched it, leaving nothing left on the ground.

"Yeah…" he said, "You wouldn't believe the technology we've got now…Since you've been here, there are new machines. We've been able to triple our yield on moon systems." He flipped through the notebook. "It's amazing really. You won't believe the statistics." He moved towards his rocket ship.

"Here…" Isabella got up and said quickly. "Follow me…" stopping him halfway back to his ship, to his radio. With an urgency in her voice, she said, "There's something I need to show you."

Back to the wall of blackberries and then into the winding, he followed her down a twisting steep path. She took him under vines the size of tree branches. Other paths criss-crossed and then squeezed on through the sharp maze. She could open doors in the green which led to other dark hallways.

When he turned on his helmet light, she finally laughed.

"This is not exactly following company specifications, Isabella." An entire world had been tunneled out of the planet. He was lost and tired, cramped after a long shuttle flight to this small moon and now she had him walking miles in the crop. In places all he could see was her shadow on the narrow trail in front of him. It was hard work keeping up with her. "What did you want to show me?" he called. He stopped. The thorns were tearing his suit. "Isabella? Where are you?" he repeated, but his words were getting to no one. Blackberry grew above him and around him. She had planted him like a seed.

Jack and the Sunflower

For five minutes every morning, the singing would stop. Jack lay there in bed awake and wondered where all the birds went from 5:02 until 5:07, when, like a magic act, they always reappeared, filling the garden air. Something small in minutes occurred that only someone who doesn't sleep would notice. Then the sky got lighter, the birds were singing again, with the mystery unsolved.

During the daylight hours, he was a shepherd, his sheep were his children, splashing and playing and swimming in the pool. Jack watched their little bobbing heads in the shallows while he sat in his white plastic chair and kept track of them. When they all lined up, with their orange kickboards plunging to the other side and back, Jack stood up and kneeled by the edge. He had really tried to be a good shepherd, but it kept with him that the boy had drowned. Sometimes, he didn't trust himself. Ever since the tragedy he was scared of this part and he kept close to the water, ready to move instantly. The pool suddenly turned very ocean blue and dangerous. In it, he counted them and watched them thrash in slow motion. It took only a second for something really bad to happen. Not until they all passed safely to where they could stand, could he sigh away the lifeguard panic.

When Jack got home from work, the witch was in the garden, he could see her bending back in the green as she weeded. All kinds of medicines, herbs, vegetables and flowers grew around her.

As Jack became more alone, hurting to himself and sad from the accident, the dark confusion only went away when he saw her. She was his connection to life. He stopped thinking about the job and leaned over the fence to watch her care for the garden. He could feel that she knew what he needed too.

"Hello," she smiled. Her fingers kneaded the dirt around some little purple flowers he saw coming up. She put some water on them and spoke to them and Jack too. "Perennials," she said. "They wouldn't want you to think they've been forgotten. So every spring at this time and place, they reappear."

"Yes," Jack said, watching from the fence, "I like them."

She stood up to look down on them happily. "The ground is like another world, so many things pass through it, living and dying. Coming out to see us," she bloomed her long fingers, "then disappearing for a while."

He needed to hear her voice talk about the things like that. He quietly nodded, looked down and touched the bean growing on vines next to him.

She moved carefully along the stones patterned into a winding path. "Have you ever seen a sunflower grow so fast?" she asked. The winter was just barely passing, but in the center of the yard, it stood nearly three feet tall. At the top was a flower grilling like a big orange plate. Still, he only noticed these things when she showed him.

She brushed through the crowd of morning glories and foxglove to stand next to it. The petals hovered near her waist. "There's something strange about this one." A few seconds passed as she stared. "We'll have to keep our eye on it."

Jack actually did fall asleep that night, but soon the dreams flapped at him and woke him up, so he put on his clothes and went to the small kitchen. It's not true, he discovered, about a watched pot. He had all the time in the world to watch the water on the stove go from cold to boiling bubbles. Then he poured and instantly had coffee to hold and drink, looking out the black window.

Day begins the same way, it happens so slowly, the sky becomes blue so creepingly that only someone used to watching and waiting would know. There were more cups of coffee inside of him. He could see the garden below in a fog of shadows, and his alarm clock ticked near him, closer and closer to the hour. Birds had started to be awake, one by one. From days of listening, he knew exactly when they would stop and today he would see what happened.

Five o'clock arrived. He kept watching the long hour hand and the new dawn light in the garden. Then it began to happen, the small birds singing from all over the place began to pour to the center of the backyard, landing around the sunflower and some of them perched like buttons up the stalk.

Jack knew it was 5:02, when the air went silent. He could see it happening from his window, the flower became a yellow face and it opened its mouth and drank all the birds inside. The golden cheeks puffed, holding its breath, keeping them all in for five minutes. Even from upstairs looking down, Jack recognized the face of the flower. At 5:07, the boy exhaled slowly, letting the string of birds out, to start singing in the world again.

THE 1943 LITTLE PIGS

"You think Twig is going to get away?"

Potts shook his head. His attention was on driving the stolen car fast. There were crops on either side of the road, strawberries for acres.

"He should have stayed with us. I don't see how he can get away on foot."

Bilder held the bag full of bundled money on his lap. "Once we get this divvied up," Bilder said, but Potts cut him off, turning on the radio. A classical orchestra played.

Potts tried to turn the station. "I don't want to hear violins," he seethed, but the button broke in his hand and the music wouldn't stop. Potts growled.

"Don't you think we're driving a bit fast?" Bilder asked as they screeched around a 20 mph turn. A watermelon bumped behind them. The whole back seat was packed with them. They hadn't cared when they stole the car.

The sedan rattled over a metal bridge spanning the river, Potts floored it on the other side. A farmhouse with a windmill blew by.

From out of a driveway overgrown with morning glory and tosses of blackberry, a black and white police car sirened onto the road in their wake.

"See! I knew it!"

"Shut up!" Potts fired. His eyes were tight in the rearview mirror. He turned the wheel violently on another hairpin turn. The crash in the back cut him a quick smile.

"What do we do?"

"Get busy with those watermelons."

"What?"

"Start heaving them watermelons out!" Potts yelled at him. The Rachmaninoff sawed like crazy on the radio.

Bilder did as he was told…Potts had got him this far hadn't he? With not the greatest of ease, the car rocking and skidding, he managed to lean over the seat and get the back window open. "Alley-oop!" he said.

The first watermelon cracked like Humpy Dumpty on the tar, and the police cruiser jerked to avoid it. Bilder could see the young policeman, one hand on the wheel, one holding the radio mic up to his mouth. "They're calling all cars," he told Potts.

"Keep tossing!" Potts barked.

Bilder must have got lucky. The fifth watermelon caught the wheel of the cruiser, and with a terrible scream of rubber and metal, it hurled into the irrigation ditch. "Bull's-eye!" Bilder lost his balance clapping his hands and fell over the seat into the watermelons. It took him a minute to get back to the front seat. They weren't on the paved road anymore—Potts had taken them down a muddy tractor lane.

"Where are we?"

"We're going to lay low."

"Good idea."

Potts tapped his forehead. "I saw this in the movies. You lay low, hide the car, then steal another car when the coast is clear. This looks like a good place to me."

Their car fit between an old barn and an ivy covered rusted thresher. Bilder had to push his door hard against it to open it. They spent the next five minutes hiding any sign of the car using whatever was around, an old wire mattress, planking, a road sign, the ruins of a rabbit hutch. Also, Potts ripped some ivy down onto the disguise.

"That'll do." Potts took the money from Bilder and they went into the barn.

It was big inside and tilted with age, the sunlight was slatted through all the broken ribs. Their feet clattered on broken shards.

"What a place…" said Bilder. He pointed to a ladder slanting to the loft. "Should we hide out up there?"

"Naw, I like the looks of that…" Potts was staring at a big kiln. An ancient stack of bricks made a dusty wall next to it.

Bilder told him, "But that's an oven."

Potts glared at him and Bilder finched. "That's a hideout."

"Okay, okay."

Potts dropped the bag full of money on the piled bricks. "Why don't you bring us in some watermelons? I'm starving."

"Alright," Bilder said, but he paused. "Do you think Twig got away?"

"How do I know? I'm not a mind reader."

If he could have seen beyond the broken walls of the barn, over the fields of strawberries and silos, parting swerves of starlings back to the town they left in such a hurry, Twig was at a ticket window, trying to play it cool.

"That will be fifty-nine dollars."

Twig dug his hand in his pocket and took out a bound stack of twenty dollar bills. He broke the paper band and pulled out three crisp Jacksons. His hand was shaking, they were both aware of it. "I have a cold," he said.

The teller grabbed a microphone off his desk and shouted, "Police! He's over here!"

Bilder shook his head. "I hope he made it. He's not a bad guy."

"He's a bum. Get the watermelon, we got to set up for a stake-out."

"Stake-out?" Bilder should have known better, he should have never been here to begin with. Too bad, he could have done this job on his own without these two bumbling partners. Or he could have been a stenographer.

"Watermelon!"

"Okay, okay." Bilder walked into the sunlight.

"Freeze!" Two policemen pointed guns over a black and white hood.

Bilder stood there, still, like a scarecrow as the police took him to the car.

"Where's your partner?"

Bilder bumped his head on the car getting pushed into it. "You won't get him." He knew that was from a movie too, he couldn't help it. He was locked in the back of the cruiser. He tapped the cage wire and asked the rookie up in the front seat, "How did you know we were here?"

The kid in the front seat, really he looked like a boy scout, pointed at the driveway. "We followed your tire tracks."

But even the kid jumped when a rattle of gunfire came from the barn. They both stared at a white barn owl flushed from the eaves. It was snow-blind. It flew without a sound in a big arc, into a waiting willow tree.

THE KIERKEGAARD READER

He opened the alley door while balancing a big cardboard box in his arms. It was filled with Marla's cassette tapes, her new recording, *Marla Povitt Sings the Ballads*. Outside without dumping the box, Stan let the door bang shut. He took the alley way out because he knew the super was sitting on the front steps. It was the first of the month. Rent was due. Stan had to creep around one more day until payday.

But he wasn't the only one in the alley. There were two shady looking guys by the dumpster. Stan just had time to see the taller one in the gray hooded sweatshirt take something and stuff it inside his coat. They scattered quickly out the other side of the alley.

Stan couldn't believe what he had seen. What had they exchanged? It looked like a tropical fish swimming in a plastic bag of water. Was that possible? Had he witnessed some illegal fish deal? It was possible he had never heard of such a thing before. Stan led a pretty quiet life. He washed dishes at a Chinese restaurant and read Kierkegaard.

At the moment he was going to work by way of Eclipse Records to see if they would take Marla's cassettes on consignment. She was his next door neighbor. He had to listen to her moaning piano through the wall. "Sure, I'll take them for you," he had told her. Little did he know what was going on out in the alley.

About to start walking for the street, he found his way was blocked.

They were back. "We decided you saw too much."

"Look," Stan tried, "I'm just carrying a box."

"Come on," said the guy who took the fish. There was no sign of it now. They came down the alley towards Stan, looking ready to tear him apart.

Stan only froze a moment, then he tossed the box at them, turned and ran the other way, out into the sunlight on the street, past the screams of his landlord trying to get lost on the avenue.

He couldn't talk to the cook about it. They only shared a few words of English. Stan had picked up a little Chinese too, but only the necessities for survival in a kitchen. He brooded in the steam, pulling out another load of clean glasses, utensils, plates and teacups. They burned his fingertips and palms as he took them one by one.

It wasn't until the afternoon, in the lull after the lunch rush, when Stan had a chance to talk with the deliveryman about what had happened.

Minor was taking the fresh produce out of the white buckets he carried in. "Oh man..." Minor said, "You don't even *know* what you saw?"

"No."

"You never heard of trop?"

"Uhh...no."

Minor sighed loudly and shook his head. He let the glass door of the fridge close solemnly. The stocked vegetables stared through the window. "I'm guessing you don't know about Melters either."

Stan shook his head.

"Man," Minor slapped his hands together, "You're lucky they didn't rip your head off. Those Melters are crazy!"

"Oh great..."

"Don't you remember that Melter they caught at the aquarium? It was all over the news."

"No. I don't read the news."

"That's right. All you read is that old book."

"Kierkegaard."

"Yeah, well let's see how that helps you when you get a Melter after you."

"Does the trop come from the fish?" Stan asked, but before Minor could answer him, the cook entered the room.

"Hey," Minor greeted him.

The chef nodded, waited for the invoice that Minor unfolded from his pocket. While the chef counted the supplies, Minor shot a look of silence at Stan.

The cook grunted and signed the paper.

"Thanks man," Minor said. He stuffed the page away and signaled Stan, "You be careful." He slipped out the screen door, let it bang.

Pinning the invoice to the clipboard on the wall, the cook nodded at Stan and went back to the kitchen in the next room. Stan could hear him in there, rattling something off to the waitress.

He wished Minor could have stayed a little longer to explain the tropical fish and Melters. That thought stayed with Stan, that worry that he was missing the knowledge that could save his life. Stan turned on a little black radio on the corner shelf next to his Kierkegaard book. The cook didn't mind the station. Gene Vincent wailed. Those three minute songs played on until his shift was done.

When Stan left the restaurant, it was getting dark. Some of the cars already had their lights on. The cold of the night bit into his water scarred hands. He didn't know who they were, but he was watching out for Melters. The street felt like it could snap into a giant snake and bite him.

The bare steps of the apartment building reminded him of the simpler fear of the morning. No sign of the superintendent out there...Maybe, Stan hoped, he could just slip through the door and get to his room unobserved and all in one piece.

Tucking Kierkegaard under his arm, he got out his key and scuffed up the cement stairs. Through the glass of the door, he could see an empty hallway and the wooden staircase that went to his room on the third floor.

Even though he was at his most vulnerable out in the open, Stan managed to get inside, creep silently across carpeting and make it to his room. He shut the door behind him and took a deep breath of relief. His exhale filled his little room with a sigh. A big window let in the blue of the night.

Only when he moved did he hear the sound of his feet push something on the floor. Down in the gloom were two folded pieces of paper that had been slipped under the door. On his bending way to them, he touched the lightswitch so he could see.

He'd been expecting that first note. It was from his landlord. *I want your rent tomorrow or else.* No signature, Stan knew.

The second note was from Marla. Suddenly he felt even worse. He remembered throwing her box of cassettes at the Melters. He groaned as he unfolded it to read her flowery writing.

Stan! So much has happened since you took my music. 1—I have a show tonight at Jazz Alley! 2—I have an agent! 3—I actually heard a song of mine played on the radio! I can't believe it! I feel like I'm in a dream. And it's all because of you! Please try to come to the show at 9 if you can. I'll dedicate a song to you! Thank you so much Stan! Lots of love, Marla

Stan shook his head in amazement. He took the notes to the kitchen and placed them on the counter. He read hers again while he filled the saucepan with tap water. He put the pan on the burner and dialed a blue gas flame under it. A laugh crept out of him. *What a joke*, he thought. Those Melters had made her a star. They must have friends in high places.

But shouldn't I warn her? he worried. He was hoping to sit in his chair and read Kierkegaard tonight. That's what he liked to do. No, he knew he had to tell Marla what he had done. She could be in danger if she got mixed up with Melters. He dropped a teabag in the water and covered the pan.

The Bird Watchers of Akron

The bird watchers of Akron first reported it in the *Beacon Journal*. Someone was painting black iron crosses on cardinals. They had been spotted by several people. The red birds would glide in low out of the cold gray sky. The birders offered a reward for anyone getting a photograph. Around their table at Denny's on Thursday morning, they decided they needed a detective to discover the bird artist.

Ernie Nelson was all on fire, gulping coffee. "What kind of maniac would paint on a beautiful bird?"

The others at the table looked glumly at their plates. Not much was left. Vera had a half piece of rye bread toast that everyone kept eyeing.

"You don't need a detective! I'll find this monster myself."

"Come on Ernie…"

"Be calm, this is a job for a professional."

But Ernie held up his hands like a saint. "Give me two days."

When Ernie left the restaurant a few minutes later, he felt like an Atlantic Tern. He breathed the air and soared over the tar. On the horizon it looked like it was going to rain.

He had inherited his grandmother's car, a mustard yellow 1972 Duster. He liked it. He believed it gave him a TV detective look when he drove it around.

He let himself in. The car started after a couple of tries. *It's these cold mornings,* he thought, *I'm the same way.* Before he set the car moving, he dialed the radio to find some good music.

He got on West Market Street and drove. As the city got lower, he watched the sky, the grids and lines of telephone wires and the birds on them. He counted flocks of crows and followed those swerving patterns the starlings make.

He would let his instinct guide him. Two days gave him plenty of time.

Plus, he knew a few things about cardinals—for example, he knew the range of a cardinal's territory. He already thought this thing out. After talking with three of the witnesses, he put his high school math to good use. Plotting the intersection of the three sightings placed the cardinals in the Fairlawn district.

To avoid a bad song, he turned the station and hit the Don McChord update. Ernie was instantly smiling at that gravelly old voice on the radio. For sixty years Don McChord had been announcing the news. Ernie was just in time to hear the reporter wrap it up.

"And finally, in Akron, Ohio…Can you believe a new bird has been discovered? It's got the local bird watchers scratching their heads. See, it looks like a cardinal, but it has the markings of the World War One Red Baron plane. This is Don McChord and that's the news today."

Ernie turned the radio off. He rolled the window down. With half interest he spotted a pair of mourning doves on a TV antenna. He couldn't believe it—Don McChord had used them for the joke at the end of the report.

He stopped at the traffic light on Trunko Road. Drumming his fingers on the wheel, he waited for the green. A blue jay hopped across the top of someone's fence. He was really giving the sky the once over now, looking for red as bright as the traffic light over the road. It was about time to park and take it on foot. He had binoculars in his glovebox.

When the car behind Ernie honked its horn, he steered the Duster straight two blocks then took a left, into the side streets. He wanted trees, big yards, bird feeders. Samuel's house was nearby. Vera lived down this way too…She probably saved that toast for her birds…He kind of liked Vera, he'd been to her house a few times for tea and talk about migrations. He was thinking about her as a flash of red shot across the street. Too late, it was gone into branches around a blue house. It was time to park.

He pulled in beneath a big chestnut tree. There were sparrows on the branches, by summer this would be a deep green shaded pool. He grabbed his binoculars and got out.

It was a quiet street, bird songs, the clack of an aluminum ladder some guy was setting up against his house. Ernie was close to a cardinal, he could feel it.

He drew the binoculars around his neck and started walking. He whistled a cardinal call and tried it again. It was better the second time. He paused to listen for an echo. Bird watching meant being a detective, having powers of deductive reasoning and a long knowledge of the subject to draw on.

The ladder creaked as the man on it turned to ask Ernie, "You looking for something?"

"Oh." Suddenly he felt suspicious, standing there on the cement with binoculars. "I'm looking for cardinals."

The man took a step down the ladder.

Ernie cracked a smile. "You probably have a pretty good view up there."

"I read that story in the paper too," said the man on the ladder. "Are you after the reward?"

"No. I'm...Actually I'm trying to find the person who painted the cardinals. I'm a detective."

"Uh -huh." The ladder creaked again. He pointed, "Well, you might start by looking around the corner there."

"Okay. Thanks. I will."

Something flickered by in the air. Ernie twitched. It was only a yellow finch. It did look like a toy airplane though. He could almost understand why someone would paint them that way.

He followed the cracked pavement, turned on the next street, watching all the places a bird could be. A lane of cherry trees lined the street, their pink blossoms were only a day or two in unfolding. He wondered if that was why the man on the ladder had sent him this way, to see this postcard of spring arriving after the long cold Ohio winter. He paused. There were sparrows hopping in the branches.

Then, it was exactly like one of those television programs, his breath caught, he could almost hear the fanfare as time seemed to freeze the moment. He had discovered the final clue that broke the cardinal mystery.

There was a wooden sign hung to the gate of a yard.

I Paint Anything
Houses, Pictures
Birds

And as if directed with bird choreography, a cardinal dropped out of a tree and landed on the lawn. It tucked its painted wings to its sides.

In less than an hour Ernie had found the place. He felt like the hero in a short story by Raymond Chandler...stepping from the umbrella of new cherry blossoms, pushing open the wooden gate, walking on the slate of flagstones towards the culprit's house.

Actually, he hadn't prepared a victory speech. At breakfast, he pictured himself in a damp garage pummeling a sallow looking teenager. Now that he was here, the fight had gone out of him, his temper had cooled. Also, he didn't expect to find himself in a garden like this. He slowed to a stop on the path so he could stare and take everything in. A museum was grown around him.

"Hi, Ernie!"

He knew her voice, though in his head he just couldn't picture her being here, until he saw her, standing on the porch.

"You really are a detective," Vera laughed. She stepped down into the grass next to a tiger sculpture made from strips of tin. "Do you know Charles Deloney?"

"No." Ernie watched the front door open, and a big curly haired man walked onto the porch. His blue overalls were speckled with paint.

"Hey. I'm Chuck."

"Hi," Ernie said. "He's the one who painted the cardinals?" he asked Vera. "Why didn't you tell me?"

She twisted her mouth and looked away.

The artist held up his big hands apologetically, "It was just an idea I had. I stopped doing that a long time ago. I heard about the trouble I caused with those birds. Sorry."

"Sorry?" Ernie had stuffed his hands in his pockets. The car key fit in his palm. He closed a fist around the key and sighed.

A HUNDRED BIRDS

The storm had finally rolled away. It left a bruise on the horizon when he got to work and surveyed the windy damage. Branches were thrown across the ground and over a roof, a wire lay down. He hoped nothing got out of the cages.

The buffalo were there. As he drove by, two monkeys clung to their tree like overripe fruit. Their tire pendulum swung with no one on it. The chickens were feather beaten. The tortoise was a stone in his field. But the giraffe was dead. The thunder must have made it run without sense enough to halt at the fence.

He stopped beside it and turned the engine off. The long shape of the giraffe ran through the weeds like a checkered African river. He would need to do something.

So he did.

Every bump or turn in the road, he looked in the mirror to make sure the trailer was still attached. The giraffe lay heavily across the bed of the truck, all the way to the extremity of the boat trailer where its head dipped sorry opened eyes.

Getting the giraffe to the lake unseen and then backing down into the water to float it away sounded like a dream, but in the new calm light of morning after the storm, he met only a few doves on wires watching him. Tall walls of corn on either side sheltered him from farmers' eyes.

He fiddled with the radio dial nervously...country music, religious monologues and their commercials, but no newsflash reports. He gripped the wheel with both hands and steered the rest of the way there.

The lake shimmered ahead of him. It was wide and deep enough to hide any mystery with waves and silt or carry the pieces away. He turned around in the empty parking lot and maneuvered the giraffe towards the boat ramp. Lined up, he shifted the truck again and started to reverse. The water held the wheels when he stomped on the brake.

Children had poured out of the wildflowers and sand to run up and stand next to his door. He cut the motor and greeted them. A wave was all he could manage.

"What's going on?" the first one had to chirp. "Is that a real giraffe?" and "Why is it on your truck?" and very soon the air fairly sang with their questions. It was a hundred birds until their teacher hushed them. She wore binoculars around her neck. She read the message on the green door of his truck and asked, "Are you from the zoo?"

"Yes."

"Maybe you could explain to the children what you are doing."

A girl said, "What will happen to the giraffe?"

"Well…" he stalled. He could hear the water lap at the trailer. He came that close. "This giraffe had an accident in the storm last night."

The children let out a sad chorus.

"Don't worry! It's happened before." He quickly tried again, "It will be alright. I drove him here to dip him in the lake. It's the only thing that works to restore a giraffe."

They stared at him.

"You need a lot of water," he continued. "Everything will be alright though," he waved, "you can go back to your fieldtrip now!"

The teacher laughed. "Oh, I think the children will find this far more interesting than any redwing blackbird." They clamored like a tin marching band.

He tried to smile. He said something under his breath as he restarted the truck. "Why not…" he shrugged.

He turned to watch over his shoulder as he backed the giraffe into the lake.

The silver water rippled over savannah camouflage.

Probably a minute pushed by before he dared to speak. "Sometimes these things take time." It was plain to see how the teacher felt about what her class of eight year olds might be witnessing.

"Is the giraffe asleep?" a little voice asked.

He rubbed his forehead to wake any answer that would help. Nothing. It didn't matter though.

A splash and four legs thrashing kicked at the trailer and threw the truck from side to side. The giraffe had returned to life and flung itself off into the water. Screaming children scattered as they hid in the weeds and dunes.

He leaped out of the truck cab, falling back in time to catch the breeze and spray of the giraffe crashing past him.

Its tall neck angled off.

He saw it go, in the few seconds it took to disappear over the hill. It left a path riddled with redwing blackbirds.

PASSING THROUGH PERU

Relaxed and sitting in the dark booth with his back against the wall, he breathed calmly as they had told him to do. "Kathmandu," he said. The Astral Projector whirred to life, the round lens poured white light into him. It was so bright he shut his eyes. That was okay they said. "Kathmandu," he repeated.

It didn't take long before a movie started. A beautiful woman appeared and prepared him for the journey. She told him he was leaving. He followed her waved silk sari. He was going.

The world hissed below him, like standing on a sandy shore with the water pulling back to sea running through your toes. Then he opened his eyes, he wanted to see the golden rocket he was flying in.

Right away, Roland knew he made a mistake. He was falling. "What's happening?" he called. Where was she, that beautiful woman?

Her image spun in close for a moment. "You weren't concentrating," she told him and she dissolved.

"Great," he said. The falling sensation suddenly stopped, he landed, but it was black. He wondered: *Was it nighttime?* Or…No…His eyes had been closed. He laughed as he opened them.

It was a sunny warm day. He had to shade his vision with his hand. Where was he? Green was all around him. He was planted in a field like a tree.

Two kids, a boy and a girl, stood next to him eating ice cream cones. It was a hot day somewhere and they were staring at a man who appeared from nowhere.

"How's the ice cream?" Roland asked.

They stared. He felt like he was starring on their TV.

"Is it good?"

The boy, he must have been about seven, answered, "Yes."

The little girl just stared at him, eating her ice cream. It was vanilla. Her face was painted white by it.

"You here to go fishing?" the boy asked him.

Roland was still bewildered. He hadn't completely taken in his surroundings. The pond was about a hundred feet wide, set in a wide green yard. There was a house not far away, a windmill that wasn't turning, a few big white clouds in the blue sunny sky.

"Fishing?" Roland repeated. Of course…He saw the sign next to the pond. You Catch Lagoon, it read. There was a rowboat tied to a door-sized dock.

The kids stared at him still.

"Yeah, sure. I'll go fishing. Why not?"

The boy had been waiting for that. "Come on," he said. He and the girl led the way to the water's edge.

What happened to Kathmandu? Roland wondered. Would he suddenly be whisked back into the ether to arrive there? He hoped so. Meanwhile, he decided to pretend this was a dream between dreams.

"Where are we anyway?" he asked the boy. "I mean, what town is this?"

"Peru," the boy said.

The little girl repeated it, "Peru."

"Peru." Roland was sure it was America though. Wasn't it?

The boy stopped beside the boat. He passed his cone to his sister to hold. "You stay there Caroline. You know you can't come out on the water."

She plunked obediently on the sun worn boards. Ice cream dripped on her shirt from her arm.

"You can get in, mister."

"Do you know what state Peru is in?" Roland asked as he sat on the bench. The boat sunk nearly to the mud. Once you looked past the reflected clouds, you could see through to the bottom of the pond. It wasn't deep.

"Ohio." The boy wanted to row Roland. He held the oars outwards like a praying mantis and with a slap they hit the water. Another hit, and they went further out.

A couple of trout drifted past, so slowly Roland felt he could have reached into the pond and easily grabbed one. There were other fish too, pike or walleye, all sizes drifting by like tame livestock.

The boy paddled on, the boat responded with a casual weave back and forth.

"You want me to fish with this?" Roland asked. A toy-looking fishing pole lay at his feet. It was orange plastic with a yellow reel.

The boy said, "I caught plenty with that."

"Okay."

"Most people catch their limit right away."

Roland picked up the toy rod and weighed it in his hand. "What do I use as bait?"

The boy stopped his ragged rowing. They were in the middle of the pond. "You don't even need bait." He smiled. There was an ice cream moustache on his lip. "You just cast it out. You'll see."

"If you say so..." He had taken a bad bounce in Peru. Roland hoped he would be in the air again soon. The fishing pole was about a foot long, Roland held it foolishly and gave it a flick. The line tumbled out a yard or so, and stopped at the end of its spool. The silver metal weighted hook dropped with a plop into the sky blue water.

Immediately, the surface of the pond frothed and slashed with fish. Roland held on tightly to the rod as the cartoon piranha frenzy whipped the line back and forth. The pull got more and more ferocious as if bigger fish after bigger fish were taking the lure, devouring each other like a crazy food chain.

"Hold on, mister!" the boy cried.

The boat was pitching. Roland had his feet dug into the hull when he saw the shiny fish break the surface and roll. Big as a car, it grabbed the bait and ran. Roland didn't have time to let go. He was in the air—he was driven underwater—it was dark and he was cold and spinning.

There didn't seem to be another second passing before he was sitting on a balcony with his back against the wall. A wind chime was ringing over his head. It must have been morning. He could hear roosters, dogs barking, all the bells and motors with chimney smoke drifting on the tilted patchwork roofs of Kathmandu.

THE REVENGE OF ETHAN FROME

After a week, Roland began to doubt he would ever get a reply. All he found in the mailbox were bills and those slick piles of advertising coupons. They must get a hundred letters a day, he thought, most of them are probably delirious drawings from children. The one or two letters like his must get lost in the shuffle.

He felt a little bad about his letter now, after all the twins were mesmerized by the program. When *The Cleveland Tennessee Show* began, they blissfully chanted along to the theme music and cheered when the puppets appeared.

Roland watched over the top of his envelope as the show continued. The manila package contained three scripts he wrote for the show. If only they would take his stories. That was his dream, to make a living writing. The only time that was his to write was late at night after all the jobs and everyone was in bed. A table by a window, paper and a pen…These scripts were part of his dream, like the faint far off rattle of a late night train swooping past sleeping houses.

Once the show was over, they were ready to go again. On sunny days like this one, they would go to the park. The neighborhood had a little square of grass with a slide and swings. He dropped the envelope in the blue mailbox planted under the cherry trees. He was out there loading the boys into the swing seats when his wife drove next to the curb and waved.

He waved back. This was their half hour together, her shift at work was done, his was about to start. The twins were pumping their legs like jitterbugs, they saw her too.

They played and shared some sandwiches, then she took over the family and he went off to work.

One thing about driving a three wheeled cardboard car, he had to fight the wind to stay on the road. All the way to the library, he pulled the tiller like a sailor.

When he got there, his arms were sore. He stood up, took the line from the locker in the car's hood and tied the windblown car to the parking meter. Employees could park there for free. Anyone else had to pay by the hour. If you forgot to put coins in the meter, a little tin woodpecker would come out and peck your car.

The security guard at the door gave him the okay and Roland made his way through the library to the basement doors. Down there was his desk, piled high with a pyramid of books. The sloppy paper tower was every copy of *Ethan Frome* in the library system. It had taken him a week to collect them all.

He picked up a bruised hardbound that looked like it had spent sixty years on the top shelf sitting in weak sunlight and dust. The book didn't even want to open, it held its covers tightly together like a seashell.

"Alright then," he told the book and tossed it back on the desk. It had to happen like this. He had an extensive report on this particular title. According to records the last check-out occurred seventeen years ago.

He sat down.

He had done the math, he had figured the shelf space it would save, this was purely a budgetary matter. A library was a garden that needed thinning, that was his job. There were plenty of books that never got looked at. They might as well be blocks of wood. He reached for his buried phone and dragged it free of some paperbacks.

Now there was one last task. He opened his report to the last page and read her name, Teri Denwatz. For the record, all he needed to do was contact her and check off the box on the report.

Roland picked up the receiver and dialed her number. If she didn't have a compelling reason for saving *Ethan Frome*, all

72 copies would be permanently removed. He could file his report and go on to the next title, *Edwin Drood*.

He listened to three rings then a man answered, "Yeah?"

"Is this Mr. Denwatz?"

"I'm Marvin, what do you want?"

"I was hoping to speak with Teri Denwatz, I'm calling from—"

"She doesn't live here."

"Do you have a number where I can reach her?"

The man laughed. It sounded like he let it out of the pocket of a corpse. "You wouldn't believe what happened to her."

"What?"

Roland could hear Marvin muffling the phone. "Hey Dawn! Someone wants to hear your daughter's life story!"

Roland heard enough. He cradled the phone and pushed it back into the books. He was glad to see *Ethan Frome* go. He marked the box next to her name and shut the report. Case closed. Roland smiled. He knew he was doing good work for the library. This would be the fifth book he dismissed. As he piled them on a big book truck, he couldn't help wondering if he would finally get a raise. *Maybe*, he hoped.

With the books all on board, he pushed the truck up the ramp and pressed the door activator. The door clacked on its track, old chains and gears pulled it open revealing the dusky end of daylight. Roland got the book truck rolling again.

It was nice outside, the birds in the surrounding field sung their goodbyes to day, a cooling breeze played the leaves of the big chestnut tree. He eyed his car waiting for him. When he drove it home, it would be black on these country roads.

He pushed the books past a couple of burned circles on the cement over to Ghat #4. He couldn't remember the last book that was dismissed here. It had left behind a bird-like shadow. Carefully and skillfully as a bricklayer, Roland unloaded *Ethan Frome* onto the feathery soot remains.

With them stacked into a pyre, Roland unlatched the flamethrower from the book truck, pointed the nozzle and pulled the trigger.

From now on the novel was gone. He knew the story though. He could reenact it for the puppets on *The Cleveland Tennessee Show* if anyone wanted him to. The fire spread and took over. No more sled riding into tragedy, he watched the pile of books burn away. It reminded him of that Orson Welles movie where Rosebud burns.

Musing on that, he turned to clip the flamethrower back on the cart latch. When he looked at the fire again, he saw the breeze lift a page. It turned and seemed to flap orange white wings while he stared. This was Ethan Frome's revenge, a tumbling shard of flame that landed on his cardboard car.

Mental Magic

"Only fourteen more days until it snows," he said through his false teeth. They clicked in his mouth like river stones. Cornlin Farrot also wore a fake moustache and a coarse black wig, with a yellow baseball cap pressed on top.

The bus driver said, "Is that so?" The bus drivers knew Cornlin. Anyone riding the 150 route at this time of morning had seen him at his perch, the first seat to the right. The drivers had even given him a nickname, Mental Magic, for Cornlin had an amazing knowledge for numbers, he was like an almanac.

He pointed the thick sleeve of his green rain jacket straight ahead out the sheet of windshield. "The pancake house is closed. It was open for 22 years."

With a grin, the driver asked, "How many days is that?"

"8,030," Cornlin replied. "Soon it will be a Mexican restaurant. When it opens, I'll have to go."

As the bus passed the blank concrete building, Cornlin turned in his plastic seat to watch. The dark glasses he wore hid his eyes. The sight of it seemed to remind him of something else, something that quieted him. Some mornings Cornlin would go on and on like a radio, but now he seemed preoccupied, weighed down by a heavy thought he wouldn't share.

For the rest of the ride he remained silent, clutching his blue cloth shopping bag on his lap, staring at the window. When the bus stopped and the door clacked open, he stood up and left without saying goodbye.

The driver watched Mental Magic get lost in the streetlights and shadows. Maybe tomorrow he'd ask him if he was doing okay.

Cornlin's shuffling walk across the damp stone pathway of campus began to change the moment he opened the glass door of Accounting Services. Once inside, it was like another pair of legs was walking him, taking him swiftly down the hall, around the corner to the men's restroom, out of sight. True, he used to worry about being spotted, but it was always early when he arrived and some time ago he had taken the precaution of informing the custodial staff to clean this floor last. He could make decisions like that. Cornlin Farrot was the director of Accounting Services.

He shuffled past the sinks, the wall of mirrors, and entered the furthest stall. He set the bag on the tiled floor. He took off his yellow cap and wig and hung them on the silver hook of the door. Then piece by piece he removed his bus riding disguise, replacing it with the carefully folded suit in his blue shopping bag. The false teeth he tucked into a pocket of the rain jacket. The transformation was complete. The tennis shoes were gone too. Instead, he wore expensive leather wingtips with tassels.

As he left the stall, gone too was the shuffling gambol, now he walked as if he had been starched, rolled in a fresh American flag. He stopped in front of the row of mirrors and cleared his throat.

"Redefining the academic workplace..." he said. It only took that long for him to find his voice. It was deeper, grating as an asbestos panel. "Necessarily, it has become strategically imperative at this time..." His face was set between thoughtfulness and a frown. He slipped one hand in the pocket of his suit, the other he used to jab the air. "I know we're all aware of the severity of the budgetary climate..." He paused again, rose on the tips of his shoes and settled again. He still had an hour before the staff meeting when he would announce the elimination of two staff positions. "I see this as an opportunity for reshuffling responsibilities at the job core..." He did enjoy the sound of his voice. He smiled.

Then he heard something move over in the stalls.

Cornlin caught terror in the mirrored eyes staring back at him. Someone else was in here, had been in the stall next to him the whole time, and knew of his disguise.

If it was one of the cleaning ladies, he would fire her on the spot. But what if she threatened to tell? Walking towards the stall Cornlin actually considered murder.

He stopped at the first stall. His hands had become fists. "Who's in there?" he growled.

The silver latch scratched and the door swung open.

Cornlin took two steps backwards. He was facing a gorilla.

Actually it was someone in a gorilla suit, but the scare had been just as real.

"Look..." the gorilla began, "Don't get any weird ideas. I didn't mean for anyone to find me in here..."

"Who are you!" Cornlin demanded.

The gorilla sighed, bowed and took off his head. A red faced and sweaty man in his fifties blinked at Cornlin. "Name's Marty. Marty Brickles. This is the first time I ever come in this building, Mr. Farrot. Usually I hang around the Steam Plant."

"What exactly are you doing?"

Marty shrugged. He chuckled, "Ahh, I don't know...I like to put on this costume and stomp around in the woods before work. I never hurt anyone. Every once in a while I give someone a scare, that's all. Hey, you're not going to turn me in, are you, Mr. Farrot?"

Cornlin glared.

"I know you're a big man around here, Mr. Farrot, but you don't have to say anything...Besides..." he turned the gorilla mask in his hands, stroked it like a rabbit, "I guess you got a secret too."

EUPHONIUM

Lon Tupperman cornered her in the hall and his beady eyes locked her in place. "My son's got a new record," he said. "You have to buy one."

She had heard about this son many times of course. Jerry Tupperman was 17, and the way his father carried on you would think he was the greatest euphonium player since...well, ever.

"Oh," Ruth said. "He's been working on that record for a while now?"

"It just came out. I've got a box of them. Burt already bought one."

"I don't actually have any money on me."

"That's okay, you can pay me later. Twenty bucks. I'll bring you one."

"Oh..." she repeated.

"It's brilliant. I guarantee you'll like it."

"I'm sure I will."

"Money back guarantee."

"Okay, Lon."

Lon smiled. "Okay then." He eased back a little. His hands had dropped to his side. That was all he needed to tell her.

Ruth said, "Thanks, Lon," and made her way around him. She carried her teacup and a little sealed bag of green tea, went about twenty more steps down the hallway to the big water tank planted against the wall.

She pressed the red button on the tank and filled her cup with steamy water. She knew there was no way out of it. Lon would hound her for the money. *Anyway,* she smiled, she was a sort of patron to Jerry Tupperman. After all, she had his first recital on a 45 single. His version of "Mary Had a Little Lamb" played like something hurtling out of a subway tunnel, shrieking at you full force. She had also been present on two cold Thanksgiving parades when the boy marched past with his euphonium. So yes, she supposed there was no way around purchasing his latest endeavor. She wasn't even surprised when she reached her desk to find the album waiting for her, leaning against the typewriter.

On the cover a young man rested next to a merry-go-round. He wore a purple turtleneck sweater and held a shining euphonium bundled under his arm. *Jerry Tupperman* was printed at the top, followed below by the big yellow lettered title, *Gurdies.*

"Oh boy," Ruth muttered. She set down her tea cup and sat. She glanced at the clock. *Three more hours to go...*

The time went the usual way, typing cards, adding them to filing cabinets. At 5, she was done for the day. This part was a bit of a routine too, following her coworkers out of the building, to sidewalks wet with spring rain, city crowds, her shoes clicking on the cement, going two blocks to the trolley stop. She kept the awkward sized album tucked under her raincoat and waited. Pedal cars went by tossing a fine spray into the air next to the curb, hitting puddles with a splash.

When the trolley arrived, pulled up the street by two soaking yaks, Ruth's coat shined with wet.

She crowded on, down the aisle and grabbed a post to hold onto. She held her other arm over the record, pressing it to her.

The trolley was full of office workers and merchants going home. Someone with a Victrola sat in the seat next to Ruth. The horn of the record player pressed into her whenever the trolley jolted. She thought of putting Jerry's record on and giving it a spin. The sound of his euphonium would probably send people fleeing out the door, giving her a chance to sit. It was a long ride to her stop on Mulberry Hill.

"Cedar Avenue," the driver's voice crackled from the speaker and everyone staggered as the trolley halted. Like a tide, they all fell back a few steps as more passengers got on.

Ruth held to a chair that a very old man occupied. She looked over his frail shoulder to share the book he was reading. This was one of her favorite trolley activities. Whenever she could, she would eavesdrop on someone's reading. She put the words together into an ongoing adventure in her mind, as if it was all one book. So far this week she had been a deep-sea diver, a cook preparing Irish stew, she had been in a crossword puzzle, and got lost in the cryptic jumble of the stock market, and now this: the old man held a paperback mystery up close to his chin. She was in a dark house carrying a candle before her when the trolley came to a sudden lurching stop. Ruth actually gave a little yelp. She couldn't help it, she almost fell. A baby was crying, something broke on the floor, people all over the trolley were muttering and making noise.

The very old man turned his turtle-like neck and asked Ruth, "What's happened?"

"I don't know," she said. "We've stopped." She couldn't see why though. She craned around all the trolley riders. The windows were fogged up and dotted with rain. There was no way to know what occurred until the speaker in the ceiling announced, "Ladies and gentlemen, we've had an accident." Everyone groaned. It sounded like the wind in a euphonium.

"What is it?" the old man asked Ruth, cupping his ear.

"An accident. There's been an accident."

Amid all the muttering and jostling, Ruth could feel the cool air from the door that had just clacked open ahead of her.

A man in a bowler hat, carrying an easel tipped and shoved past her, steaming for that open door. He prompted several others to abandon ship as well.

Ruth could see down the aisle, out the split screen windshield of the trolley. It was an accident all right. The yaks were feeding from the bright spray of a crushed flower stand. She could see the driver out there swatting the beasts, waving his arms. There was a woman in a blue apron shouting at him.

"Good Lord," Ruth muttered.

The driver pulled on the reins and tackle, but the yaks were intent on eating every flower in sight. No blow could sink through their thick matted hair. More people were leaving the trolley. Ruth couldn't blame them, but she still had a long way to go. She watched the family with the crying baby, followed by a boy carrying a fishbowl, all heading for the doorway. The driver wasn't having any luck. The lady in the apron held a stalk of bent iris. She was crying.

Three seats from her, Ruth saw the man with the Victrola stand up as if to leave.

"Hold on!" she called to him, having an idea and hurrying into it before it could fly away.

Carrying the record player, he turned the horn towards her.

"I think I know how to get those yaks moving again." Ruth tapped the contraption in his arms. "Can I borrow this?"

Jerry Tupperman was about to receive his greatest acclaim. Within a week, his *Gurdies* recording would be outselling everything from coast to coast. It would be played as a foghorn for ships, to clear your home of pests, a tornado alarm, or played on trolleys for misbehaving yaks.

MEMORY OF BEES

You wouldn't expect him to be a truancy officer. Terry Helms didn't look the type. He wasn't physically intimidating, he was rather portly, with pale skin that flushed easily to bright pink. Since he wasn't a threatening man, he had to use his voice, to soothe and convince when the game was over, and it was time to go back to school. With children he was like a friendly zookeeper, he just wanted them to stay where they were safe.

He waited in the rain. No, it wasn't rain, that wasn't the right word. It was drizzle. The air was wet and humid and it stuck to you like sweat. What a day for some kid to skip school. *Wouldn't you rather be inside?* he thought. Sometimes all he had to do was wander the school parking lot and look for them. Usually they just stood there bewildered by their choice of freedom. This wasn't going to be one of those days.

Like a tea kettle, the stout, round robot dropped off the metal jungle gym and clambered across the bark chips. Terry walked behind it. They were on the trail now.

For twenty minutes he walked with his robot, through neighborhoods, parking lots, across roads and off into the brush. Then the robot crawled under a cedar fence towards an old farmhouse. Behind it, in a row of poplars and a willow, was a barn that had blown down, barely holding itself up like a dog hit by a car. A faded cartoon chicken was painted on the warped leaning boards.

There was also an old woman. She sat in a wheelchair parked beside flowers.

He introduced himself, "I'm Terry Helms. I'm the truancy officer. I have reason to believe there may be a couple of school children hiding on your property."

"Good heavens!" she replied. "I can't imagine why children would want to come here."

"Who knows. Life's just a game to some of them. I hope you don't mind if I take a look."

The robot whined like a fat dog.

Terry said, "Seems like they headed over there. Is that barn safe?"

"I'm not sure. We used to keep the chickens there. That was years ago. It's not much of a chicken farm anymore. I keep a few hens and sell the eggs. Also, I teach music lessons."

That explained the flute on her lap. Terry shook his head. He said, "I better catch up with my retriever, check out that barn. I'll just cut across the field."

"You might get your feet wet."

"That's okay." He nodded to her and followed the path. The old woman creaked in her chair after him. He walked through a curtain of willow.

A wide ocean of weeds began flowing to the barn. It started shallow and got deeper. Eventually, Terry had to watch his step. An old line of fencing stopped him. He paused at the fence, one hand on the post and he called back to the woman, "Is this an electric fence?"

She cupped a hand to her ear. She couldn't hear him.

It was just a little too high for him to step over easily. It would be a terrible shock. He thought of leaping the strand but that seemed foolhardy. There was nothing to do but take a deep breath and touch the wire with his finger.

It was okay. It was cold. Terry chuckled and heaved himself over the fence, and yes, the crotch of his trousers did brush the wire so he was lucky he checked.

On the other side, his feet sunk into the loamy ground. He turned and waved to the old woman. She sat framed by drooping willow branches. She lifted her flute to return the wave.

The ground was just shy of being swampy. If he walked on the tussocks he could stay dry. It felt like hopping along the backs of turtles.

Luckily the barn was built on an elevation. A hundred years ago horse teams must have pulled the dirt up in a mound for the foundation. With one last long hop, Terry landed on the skirt of earth surrounding the barn.

His robot, splattered with mud, had already gone ahead to the dark open door.

"Hey there..." Terry called to it. "Wait up."

The barn was like a deflated wooden red balloon. The wind that had knocked it over had not quite finished the job, it seemed to be holding itself up by its elbows.

"I don't like the looks of this..." Terry muttered. He paused outside the gloomy doorway. His robot glimmered a few feet past him, waiting in the dark.

"Are you in there?" The loud sound of Terry's voice took bat shape and disappeared into the shattered wood. He took a nervous step forward, walking on the plank of gray sunlight let in. The light faded quickly.

In the gloom, Terry could see the stacks of chicken coops, could still smell their industry too. He fumbled in his coat pocket and took out a handkerchief, putting it over his nose and mouth. Muffled, he asked his retriever, "What do you think?" He could see a canoe not far away. It could easily hide a couple of runaway children.

With a sudden whirr, the robot moved off to the right near a stairway as crooked as the keys of a broken piano.

"Are you serious?" he called.

Spidery legs took the robot nimbly up the steps. Above it, the roof slanted, folded and precarious.

Terry shuffled over the cement and crumbled straw and stopped where the stairs began. The robot had left his sight.

"Hello?" Terry took another deep breath from his handkerchief and continued, "This place isn't safe..." He took a new cloth breath, "If you kids are up there, please come down." He took another breath. "You can come down and we'll go back together."

There was no reply. Terry took a flashlight from his coat and lit the crazy stairs. He put a foot on the first tipped step. His shoe crunched on a dead bee. The beam of light showed others curled up on the stairs. Maybe they were hornets. Terry pointed the flashlight above. There was a scuffed gray mark on a wooden support where the nest had been pried off.

Upstairs in the loft, his robot gave a squeak and there came a scuffling sound.

Terry shot the light across the bent lattice. Some dust shook down like fish food into a black sea.

"Who's up there?" Terry yelled. He didn't want to try those stairs. He didn't think they would hold his weight. As it turned out, he didn't have to worry about them.

As if kicked, the robot clattered and squealed down the hard steps, followed in the air by a tumbling gray shape, the softball-sized bomb of a bee hive fuzzing the air as it fell in a perfectly thrown trajectory.

Terry loped from the sight of it but all those hundreds of stinging insects were locked on him, a bumbling red glow in their intense hateful eyes. They clouded out into the daylight after him, as he ran and flapped the big brown sleeves of his coat like the wings of an owl.

Terry didn't so much feel them yet, it was all a hot burn of sudden exertion to go running, slopping over the mushy ground to the fence, flipping over, chopping his hands on his legs and neck.

When he got to the old woman, Terry could see her with the eye not puffing shut—she was trying to back away, her gnarled hands slipping on the wheels. Terry grabbed the flute off her lap. His swollen palm could barely close around it, using it as a bat, swinging at the few bees left that had made that mad dash to under the willow tree. He swatted the flute against his jacket, crushing a bug, then a few more. The air sizzled with a high pitch rill, though as Terry plucked a dead bee from his earlobe he guessed maybe it was just him.

"Oh…" he coughed.

Like a blanket snapped in the wind, it was all forgotten in a flash. The misadventure with bees disappeared as suddenly as a dream. There was no pain either, the bee memory was gone.

The old woman had gained traction and covered ground. She was stopped a few yards from him, to rest on the gravel edge of driveway. She seemed to be crying.

What happened? He left the old woman only a moment ago. Now he was here, holding the flute. Beneath his fingers, the keys on it moved.

A voice like the wind whispered through it, telling him the story. It was just like a fairy tale. Without the flute, the witch was helpless. She was already turning to dust.

He started to walk. The flute played him the way to the old woman's kitchen where Terry found the two missing children trapped in a cage made of bones. There was no sound but the flute. It filled the air while Terry got the key off a hook, unlocked their door and let them scramble out.

As they ran from the porch, the house crunched like a fist, boards, windows and chimney, wrapping itself up in the long shadows of the willow tree to hide. That might have been it except for a scratching on the ground. The robot pulled itself after them, missing legs, grinding gears, covered in mud and dead bees.

COMIC BOOK CREATURES

A girl was out in the deep hillside picking wildflowers to sell along the road. She moved slowly and steadily. When she had an armful she would turn back onto the path to pile them in the parked wheelbarrow. It was quiet work. She was caught in the wind, thinking and listening to the birds around her.

After only her second trip to harvest more, Sue heard a high pitched yellow scream come through the air. She barely had time to react as the noise became a crash that threw the ground in front of her around. The cloud of debris settled. A deafened silence punctured the spot. It was the sort of start to an adventure Sue had come to expect from reading comics and watching dreams. She crept up on the place where the air still shimmered.

She knew to be careful. Her father had warned her about rattlesnakes, how they liked to wrap half out of pits in the warm baked earth, but she didn't know much about the war, or falling stars or whatever this was.

Whatever it was shakily grew to stand up out of a flattened crush. "Ohhh my aching head...," it said, raising arms to a crumpled cowboy hat. It was a monkey, not much bigger than her. Slapping his face back and forth, he noticed her and tried to steady his wobbly gaze on her. "Who are you?" He fell back a step and jerked like a puppet on invisible strings. "Hey!" he smirked, "I'm still alive!" and he laughed with a loud, "Hah!"

Sue stood there holding the flowers, watching him.

"Hello kid," the monkey tried again. He leaned closer with a worried look, "Do you know me or something?"

"No."

"Well, that's okay then. I –" he stopped and shook the stars in his head. "Wow! That was—that was really—I'm lucky to be alive I guess..." He grinned again and pointed nondescriptly, "They shot me out of a cannon...I think they wanted to kill me..." She could see his clockwork thinking take root to his next reason, "You gotta hide me!" He lurched a few steps towards her, trampling swirls of heather underfoot. He stopped and begged, "Please kid, they'll be after me. They'll want to put my skin up for their show. They'll charge a dollar, people will pay. They'll look at me like a monster!" He panicked melodramatically. "Oh kid, have a heart, you gotta help me!" He bent his knee to touch leaf and vine.

Sue beheld his cartoon worry. Maybe she was the only one who didn't know who he was, maybe that made her his lucky break. A thought ballooned before her though and she told him, "I have a tree house. You could stay in there."

"Perfect!" he snapped.

In a little wooden planked room that let in gray and blue slats of light, the monkey sat on a pillow and chewed on his lip. "This will do..." he drawled. "I guess."

"Look," Sue chirped, "You can read my comic books." She pushed a ragged cardboard box towards him.

"Ooh! I love comics! What do you got?"

"*Little Lulus.* Some *Archies*—they're from my cousin—and *Winnie the Pooh* I like..." she paged deeper through, "*Pluto*...all kinds of stuff."

The monkey raised his eyebrows doubtfully, "Don't you have any superhero ones?"

"No. I like animals mostly. They're funny and nice. There's plenty here to read."

"Yeah? I don't know..."

"You can stay as long as you want and nobody will know you're here."

"I know...It's just...What am I supposed to do while you're out there avenging me?"

"What?"

He huffed, "It's what I told you on the way here, Sue. You have to go to the circus and get him!"

"No! I'll let you stay here, but I have to get back to work. I have to find flowers to sell, I can't go running around for you."

"You want money!" the monkey nearly shrieked. With a quick movement, he reached above under his wide-brimmed hat and pulled down some money. "Here!" he waved, "Take this! I can get more. Heck!" he shrugged, "I'd go myself, only they know me, they'd grab me right away. Pop!" He let the cash slop from his grip onto the floor. An Abe Lincoln bill flipped through the slats. "Help me out. Okay, kid?" he moped.

"Well…What do you want me to do?"

He smirked, "Oh, it's so simple. You'll see the circus— it's not so far away from here. All you have to do is buy a ticket in." He shoved money at her with his foot. "Then find that louse who shot me." He puffed himself up, "He's been planning this for a long, long time, I bet. Used to be, I thought we were partners, but look what happened!" The monkey scowled, "He's nothing but a bad old man. He's barely alive anyway. All you have to do is unplug him. His heart will give out then I can return to my circus." His eyes glittered at her like one of her comic book creatures.

Red and blue banners flapped against the perfect sky. As Sue drew near, she heard the calliope and happy cries whirred by the many stirring arms of the mechanical rides. The circus was unlike anything she'd ever seen in the valley. The spectacle had drawn people from all over and it took her another ten minutes standing in line with them to get inside.

The monkey's orders took her wandering past the hulls of tents held down with wooden stakes. Would that old man be in there, or in a caravan somewhere? Sue didn't know. She slowed.

"Don't be lost," someone in a circus uniform waved her over, "I've got what you're looking for right in here. Ever see an electric man? A mummy? How would you like to witness something kept alive by the blue light blood of electricity?"

Of course that rang a bell for her. It was what the monkey had told her, it must be him.

She gave her last dollar and went into the dark. It took her a few steps walking to get accustomed to the gloom. The racket of the circus disappeared and it was only her footsteps and heart beating.

She made for the strange something pulsing a weak glow ten feet ahead. The floor sloped towards it, subtly tipping her to the center.

A big aquarium awaited her. It emitted that blur of color in the air, along with a breathing-like hum. An illumined button read PUSH. So she did.

She watched a gray tinted film project itself inside the case. She saw armies going back and forth, cannons and rifles and explosions. Then the film repeated over again. She had seen enough, she was about to move away when the images pitched and swayed. A man sat up inside the case. That was the dollar scare.

He must have been sleeping down underneath the flow of the film. Now she noticed how the case was the size of a coffin, or an ancient Egyptian sarcophagus. Yes, and like a mummy, the figure inside the case moved jerkily, wearily, cast in yellowy light

That would have been a good carnival trick, but there was more to it. Sue recognized the lean tree-boned man in black suit, with stove-pipe hat on top. He was someone everyone in school knows.

Old Abraham Lincoln had returned through time. He moved upward creakily and stopped when his hat tapped into glass. Slowly he turned his eyes towards her and they regarded each other. His eyes glowed with warm light.

She didn't know if he was real or not, but she took a deep breath of the electric air and confessed, "The monkey told me to come here and unplug you. But I won't do it." The thought of that monkey made her furious now.

Abe held up a wooden, flat looking hand. She could have set a wildflower upon it. He calmed her down just by doing that. Everything was alright. When his eyes began to dim, he reclined back to wherever he rested, in that darkness where he lived among levers and chains, under Civil War movie reels.

VOTING

October and overnight there is fall, ice in the yellow bucket, leaves floating captured and frozen.

Inside the warm house, we finished two cups of black coffee, boiled hot for three minutes in the microwave. Going out on a morning like this meant getting prepared for the cold.

She said, "Well, I'm ready to vote. It won't take me long." She pushed her empty porcelain mug to the center of the table and wrapped a scarf on, tying the bright colors close. "Especially on that nuclear plant. They got us into this mess. I never wanted that plant to begin with." My grandmother huffed as she got up to put on some more warm clothes. Then we would go vote and change the world.

Outside. The heat of the kitchen is left behind the moment the door closes. She says goodbye to her cat in the window, looking sleepy-eyed past us watching for birds in the bare branches. "Bye, Kitty," she waved, "We're off to do our civic duty!"

A blue winter sky on a cold day.

My feet are freezing. All the ice and broken water on the street finds me.

She's in her voting day costume, warm layers of tan overcoat, lipstick and she laughs, "I got my glasses, so they think I'm spending my time voting but I already know how I'm going to vote."

Leaves fall from the trees as we walk to the school in a quiet suburb forest, past houses, sloped roofs catching leaves off trees. Sleeping through it is the distant growl of a leaf blower motor somewhere blocks away. I think about how all this should be remembered. This day is so beautiful it should be like a photograph that I can turn to anytime. She is quiet, walking, shorter than I am, next to me. Swept to the side of the road are leaves and pine needles piled like running walls.

It's recess at the school when we arrive, ball games, playing, and a kid with huge glasses looks up for a second as we pass. He is burying his hand in hibernating dirt.

My grandmother blows her nose and puts the old tissue into a pocket. She seems concerned, "Usually there's a big sign that says Vote..." She points to the chain link fence. Through the school doors, inside, down the empty halls, we feel more than a little alone until we're stopped by a man holding books.

"Voting?" she asks him. We can't understand the emptiness.

He seems shocked, as if he never could have imagined this, but he wants to be helpful. In the hollow school hallway he tells us tomorrow is voting day. "You have another day to decide."

"I know how I'm going to vote!" she persists.

But he holds the door open for us and tells us to come back tomorrow when the rest of America will be ready too.

So we leave for home, back into the cold sunny day. "This is your fault!" she jokes and we laugh about Time as a giant alarm clock that we set a day early.

A spinning ball goes past us. There are two kids are in the sand pile now. One is kneeling, blowing kazoo pitches on a straw while his friend sits packing dirt, mounding it over his hand. My grandmother laughs and stops.

"It's a straw," the boy tells her. To show the music, he toots on it loudly. He watches us wave back as we leave through his mesh school fence.

We walk on, feeling happy, even though our crusade was unsuccessful.

There's a mysterious striped cat in the road far ahead. She doesn't know who it belongs to. She tells me it's a tiger, as it slinks back into the trees, in the leaves, glancing up as we walk by. We go on, to the window where her cat sleeps behind the glass. There's a warm heater vent below. Her aquarium pet wakes up and starts meowing when we wave from the yard.

At the door, my grandmother clicks at the handle with the key. "I'll be seeing you tomorrow then." We kiss each other. "Goodbye!"

So I ride away on a creaky green bicycle that defies physics with its wobbling wheels and tempts danger with its lack of brakes.

As she opens the door, she calls to her cat. I hear the door shut behind her as I spin a cold sunny day shadow along the road.

For the second voting day, there are heavy clouds with an umbrella rain falling from the gray. Water splashes into the full yellow bucket by her door. Sunken leaves hold hands around the plastic edge.

I open the door and hear her call from inside, "I wasn't sure if you were going to make it with it raining like this!" I sit down and to prepare for the storm, we share some powerful coffee. She tells me more about her cat. "She watches the leaves. She watches the birds and trees and the people walking up and down the street. But she doesn't move. She just sits there. I think she's afraid of them." As we get ready to leave, the cat moves through the room towards the window, to watch us and wait for our return. Because of the weather, today we're driving.

In the rain, I unlock and open the garage door and when we're buckled in she backs the buzzing tiny car out. Her car is a blue Chevrolet with an engine of angry bees. The world outside is wet, the window wipers flip and wave aside the water.

There's no recess today because of the downpour, but we can see through the yellow windows where they are cutting out crayon colored shapes to tape to the glass.

Hurrying from the parking lot, we follow under the covered walkway sheltered from the rain, past the 'Vote Here' signs, up to the big entrance door. Little footprints mark the way on the white cement.

Inside there are red, white and blue streamers, flags and posters of presidents. 'Vote Here' arrows point to a row of curtained booths. Sometime since yesterday, the place had been transformed into the American Dream.

We go up to a table to get the voting ballots and the woman there shows us an example ballot. "All you have to do is connect the arrows."

So we take our ballots and my grandmother disappears behind stars and stripes curtains.

I pull aside the patriotic cloth of my booth and put the sheets on a shelf. There's a black pencil for voting, to connect arrows with.

Before me is the pink ballot form. "You vote by connecting the arrows," it repeats, with an easy to read diagram at the top.

> *Question 1: Initiative Question. Do you want*
> *to let any power plant like Maine Yankee*
> *operate after July 4, 1988, if it makes*
> *high level nuclear waste?*

I hit it with an arrow and down I went, voting on all the questions, education and taxes and the names from signs that I've been seeing in yards and all over town. When I finish sharpening arrows, I leave the curtained booth and feed my ballots into a machine that gulps them away. They have computers that can add up all the votes in only hours and overnight things can be changed.

My grandmother is waiting in the doorway. "That was quick."

"And painless," I agree.

On the way back to the exit, look who's coming—it's the same guy with all the books, the one we talked to yesterday, only now he's wearing a different sweater. "Did you vote?" He looks anxious, like he waited 24 hours watching for our return.

My grandmother smiles, nods and asks him, "Tell me. How many people showed up yesterday to vote?"

She laughs when he tells her, "As far as I know, just two."

The road reflects the sky overhead, and we drive on the clouds returning to her house.

Back in the warm kitchen, it's more cat stories, newspapers, predictions and the way of the world. Before I leave, she remembers to give me a recipe. The cat paws at the pen as she writes it for me, 'Crisp Oven Fried Fish.'

Horses

Another summer is gone. The gray is back, the rain machine is starting in gear, the wind is hissing in the tree outside our window at night. With the weight of lead, October is here and what all of this adds up to is that people turn a little desperate. You feel the passing of time, wishes are made.

My wife called the Wish Maker, it wasn't me. I don't know, sure wishes are nice, but I guess I'm not the type to get all worked up, going to the trouble of arranging for one to be made. Plus, there's all that money thrown away.

I was standing at the window watching the clouds, stirring my cup of instant coffee when there was a knock on the door.

Elizabeth answered it. We were both expecting it, but like I said, she was more excited at the prospect than I was.

"Gandy?" she said.

"That's me," laughed the voice hidden behind the opened door.

"Lenny!" my wife called me, "the Wish Maker's here!"

I was still watching the clouds. Drifts of them piled up over the islands, it looked like rain on the way.

"Will you come in, Gandy?" Elizabeth said.

"Well, generally speaking I like to do these transactions out of doors."

"Of course! Lenny, I'm going outside. Are you coming?"

"Okay…" I said. "I'll meet you. I'll get my shoes."

She shut the door. Their voices were smudged by the walls and muffling leaves of the thick rhododendron pressed to the house.

I took my coffee cup back to the kitchen, set it on the formica table and fetched my shoes from beside the back door. I had only been home from work for an hour.

Outside, I followed the sound of their voices, around the back of the house on the cracked cement path between the garage to the driveway. Some of the wet spindly flowerless stalks grabbed at me.

I could hear Gandy laughing. In another moment I could see him. He stood leaning against a tall bamboo pole, the end of it up in the air was fitted with the copper lantern that would provide Elizabeth's wish. Gandy himself didn't seem that imposing, dressed in gray sweatshirt and dark jeans. He noticed me and nodded.

My wife was telling him how much this wish meant to us.

I stopped near them and stared up at the Wish Maker's lantern.

It looked pretty beat up. There were scratches and dents on it like maybe he'd been using it to catch bats with.

"Alright," Gandy said when my wife was finished, "Are you ready?"

"Oh yes!" she cried. She quickly handed him a thick roll of money and he lowered the lantern by slanting the stick uphill.

I've never actually seen one of these lanterns up close before. Elizabeth has done this before. She even credited a Wish Maker for her finding me. I guess that's possible. I don't know. I suppose a machine could know where I would be at any given time and send me a signal to lock eyes with a girl. Who knows how love begins?

Gandy flipped a latch on the lantern and stuffed the money inside then raised the thing skywards. *Say goodbye to all that dough*, I thought. Elizabeth watched the lantern start to glow, like a girl at a circus show.

Gandy chuckled and said, "This'll be a good one."

Some of the blue white light buzzed through the cracks in the lantern. It gave a wheeze then with a pop, a spark flew out of the top, turning into a puff of acrid black smoke.

Gandy guffawed.

Elizabeth clapped her hands. I was glad the gently swooping branches of the alder hadn't caught on fire.

"You got your wish," Gandy said.

"Where?" said Elizabeth. "Where is it?"

Gandy squinted and nodded and took in a loud breath of air. "It's over behind your garage." He pointed. "In the backyard..."

"Oh Lenny!" Elizabeth grabbed my arm. "Let's go see!"

"Sure," said Gandy. He laughed again. With his tall walking stick and lantern and charcoal clothes, I got it now—he looked like a woodcut from a Grimm's fairy tale. Someone drawn in the background while the Pied Piper ran off with the children, or a troll guarding a gate to the woods. He was still chuckling as Elizabeth dragged me up the gravel driveway.

It was starting to rain lightly. Maybe there would be something practical waiting for us, I hoped, like a door going to a warmer world.

A blue jay squawked out of our way.

I don't know what Elizabeth was hoping for, but I had my hopes up too, I'll admit. The Wish Maker put on a pretty good show.

Along the edge of the garage a bright little creek of runoff water rippled downhill. It made a silver sound.

As Elizabeth and I turned the corner, we both sort of turned to stone. There in our backyard stood the sorriest looking wish I've ever seen. A horse, maybe gray at one time, it was turned to a shade of almost blue. Every angle and edge of it was crooked or bent like it had been crumpled by a big hand. When it turned to look at us, it did so with the cross-eyed gaze of a broken clock.

While I wanted to laugh at the pure absurdity of it, I couldn't. When Elizabeth let go with a sob I put my arm around her. "It's alright," I said. I could feel the rain on my neck as I kissed her hair. I looked over her at the shape in our yard. The rain made dots on the horse like swiss cheese. "It's not that bad…"

Elizabeth wiped at her eyes with the back of her hand.

"I don't know much about horses," I told her, "Maybe that's a good one."

"Yeah, right," she said.

"Well…I do think we should get it out of the rain. Let's put it in the garage?" I didn't know.

Elizabeth agreed. "You do it though."

I said, "Okay." There was a rope looped around the horse's neck. "Hello fellow," I said. It didn't seem to mind my approaching it, or maybe it hadn't seen me yet. Anyway, I got there and took hold of the rope. I wasn't afraid of it, but I didn't know what it was capable of doing. It was like a badly wired electric blanket, shivering wet. "Okay…Come along…"

I tugged and the horse started to move. I called down the hill, "Hey Elizabeth, do you think you could open the garage door for us?"

She hurried away as I led the horse across the weeds and fallen leaves. It picked up speed. By the time we got to the driveway and started down it, I had adapted to the beast's strangely irregular gait. The frequency had transmitted down the rope into me. Like the horse, my left foot kicked out a little to the side, while my right dragged at the heel.

I heard the big garage door go up with a racket of rusted coasters and my wife's groan. It wasn't easy to move that slab of metal. One of these days I had to fix it.

Fortunately our horse walked right in. Elizabeth pushed the lawnmower aside to make space. It wasn't much of a stall, but how much room did a horse need anyway? Didn't they just stand there? I ran my hand over its damp, rough back to brush off the rain. "Do we put a blanket on it?" I asked Elizabeth. I remember in *Black Beauty*, the horse got wet and they forgot to put a blanket on it and the horse got sick…Or maybe you're not supposed to put a blanket on it? I guess I can't remember…

Elizabeth rubbed at her eyes. "Lenny, I don't know anything about horses." She stared at me desperately. "I don't know what to do! I never should have called that Wish Maker."

She was right, but I wasn't fool enough to say that. The three of us stood there and listened to the rain hit the roof overhead. What were we supposed to do? Later I could take the horse back outside. There was grass in the mossy backyard. I could show it to the mountain of blackberries growing on the property line. Or were blackberries something only a goat would eat?

I sighed and sat down on an overturned bucket. It was only the start of a long season of wind, rain and cold until finally the sun would come back out again. In the meantime, I'm trying to see something golden in what happened. It could be the laughing Wish Maker Gandy was a lesson after all. We don't know anything about horses yet, but we have all winter to learn.

THE $500 FOOL

Someone was sitting on his favorite bench. Any time it was a sunny day, he took his lunch break there. His walk slowed. Twenty feet away he noticed she was drawing the water tower he liked so much. With a big pad of paper on her lap, there next to her on the bench was a china dish of water, two paint brushes slanting out. She was finishing her third picture on the page.

"Hi," she said. She colored rust onto the old steel legs and pot belly of the picture. "It's hard to believe it's going to be gone tomorrow..."

"What? What do you mean?"

"The tower is getting demolished. I'm trying to get as many pictures of it as I can before it falls down."

He tried to imagine it gone...he could, but he didn't want to. He stuck his foot next to a dandelion and stared down the hill at the old water tower. Then he looked back to her sketchpad. Six pictures of it fit on the sheet of paper. Beside her sat a stack of more.

After a silent while watching her, he asked, "You know I get the feeling you're going to run out of paint and water before too long. Will you let me go to the store and get you some more?" He surprised himself asking her that. The words had flown out of him on their own and had sent him on a mission into town. He almost felt something more than him was moving him, taking him into the Ben Franklin store where he would find what he needed.

By the time he got the four foot long roll of paper, watercolors and a plastic bottle of water onto the counter, he was feeling more like himself, especially as he took out his wallet to pay.

The old cashier gave his purchases an odd look and asked him, "What are you doing? Painting something?"

"I'm painting a giraffe," he told her. He took the little plastic bag and tucked the long paper roll under his arm like a bazooka and left the store.

The moment he was back outside though, he was doing something unexpected again. He crossed the street and went to the bank.

She was an artist. Even if the markers of our existence fail or fall apart, art continues. He left the warm day and entered the air conditioned room. He didn't have to stand in a line. He walked right up to the window and told the teller he wanted five hundred dollars in cash. That was almost all he had. He asked for it in hundreds. He stuffed them in the paper bag with the white plastic paint set and water bottle.

Watching him, the teller said quietly, "We're not really allowed to ask our clients what they're doing with their money, but I'm dying to know. Vacation?" The teller waited with a wooden grin for a reply.

"I just wanted to tell people I robbed a bank," he said and he left.

He wondered what she would do with all those pictures of the water tower. At the rate she was going, there would be a lot of them before tomorrow, enough to tie them together and string them a mile into the wind if she wanted to. He crossed the parking lot, left the street to follow a weedy path shortcut. He passed buttercups and those spindly Queen Anne's lace. How many pictures would there be? For some reason he thought of 517. Maybe it was connected to the money in the bag. 517, that's about a dollar a sketch, if you want to think of it that way. He didn't know what to think of it, he didn't know what he was doing, he felt like he was giving in to something bigger than himself.

When he got back to the park, there she was, on his bench. He set the roll of paper and the bag beside her, next to her stack of pictures. What would she do with 517 watercolors of the tower? They were like the frames of a movie, a movie where the camera never moved, it just noted the change in light from day to night.

"Are you going to get tired of the same view?"

"No," she said. "I like staring at something for a long time. It's like meditating." She was calm with her drawing. He could tell she would go on as long as she could. And what a surprise she would have when she ran out of colors and reached into the bag.

He didn't want to stay much longer. He felt like a different person, his life felt like a Charles Dickens movie. "Well, I better be going," he said. "I have to get back to my job."

"Oh..." she stopped. "You have to take this picture." She tore the paper corner. "This is the one I started when you appeared."

It was perfect. She had drawn the tower like a sapling with yellow light and a herd of pigeons making a saintly halo around it.

He put the paper in his pocket. He had to go. He had to go before she knew. Besides he was probably late. Nobody seemed to notice too much if his lunch hour ran a little over, but this had been an adventure. It could be 2:30 by now. He didn't even own a watch, or see a clock. He was rushing through the park in a dream. The blue sky and sun were over him.

Allen Frost lives with his family in Bellingham, Washington. He works at the library of Western Washington University. He is the author of six books of poetry and fiction and is currently working on a new book of poetry.

"These stories were written over the space of 24 years from Maine to New York, Ohio and on the west coast again. Despite all the time it took for this book to grow, I'm hoping you will see these 39 stories as connected chapters. I also like to think of them as episodes in some strange late-night television show. I spent a fair number of evenings watching *Outer Limits* and *Twilight Zone* and those sci-fi movies hosted by vampires. You sit there in that blue glow and suddenly you're on a planet of blackberries, or running down the street with Pal Tack."

Bird Dog Publishing
Bottom Dog Press

The Wonderful Stupid Man by Allen Frost
978-1-933964-64-5 190 pgs. $15

Dogs and Other Poems by Paul S. Piper
978-1-933-64-45-4 74 pgs. $15

The Mermaid Translations by Allen Frost
978-1-933964-40-9 136 pgs. $15

Home Recordings: by Allen Frost
978-1-933964-24-9 124 pgs. $15

Faces and Voices: Tales by Larry Smith
1-933964-04-9 136 pgs. $15

Second Story Woman: A Memoir of Second Chances
by Carole Calladine
978-1-933964-12-6 226 pgs. $16

256 Zones of Gray: Poems by Rob Smith
978-1-933964-16-4 80 pgs. $15

Another Life: Collected Poems by Allen Frost
978-1-933964-10-2 176 pgs. $15

Winter Apples: Poems by Paul S. Piper
978-1-933964-08-9 88 pgs. $15

Lake Effect: Poems by Laura Treacy Bentley
1-933964-05-7 108 pgs. $14

Depression Days on an Appalachian Farm: Poems
by Robert L. Tener
1-933964-03-0 80 pgs. $15

120 Charles Street, The Village:
Journals & Other Writings 1949-1950 by Holly Beye
0-933087-99-3 240 pgs. $16

Bird Dog Publishing
A division of Bottom Dog Press, Inc.
PO Box 425/ Huron, Ohio 44839
Order Online at:
http://smithdocs.net/BirdDogy/BirdDogPage.html

CPSIA information can be obtained at www.ICGtesting.com
Printed in the USA
BVOW010829101212

307758BV00002B/40/P